The
Ugly Princess
and the
Wise Fool

The Ugly Princess and the Wise Fool

Margaret Gray

illustrations by Randy Cecil

Henry Holt and Company • *New York*

This book would never have come to be without its brilliant editor, Reka Simonsen. I would also like to thank the Gray, Mittleman, and Steinberg families, particularly my parents, Paul and Betsy Gray; my brother, David Gray; and my husband, Harry Mittleman.

Henry Holt and Company, LLC
Publishers since 1866
115 West 18th Street, New York, New York 10011
www.henryholt.com

Henry Holt is a registered trademark of Henry Holt and Company, LLC
Text copyright © 2002 by Margaret Gray
Illustrations copyright © 2002 by Randy Cecil
All rights reserved.
Distributed in Canada by H. B. Fenn and Company Ltd.

Library of Congress Cataloging-in-Publication Data
Gray, Margaret. The ugly princess and the wise fool /
Margaret Gray; illustrations by Randy Cecil.
p. cm.
Summary: When plain-looking Princess Rose longs for the beauty to
snare handsome Prince Parsley, and the wise fool Jasper longs to restore
wisdom to the kingdom, they end up working together and find
they must face the magical Godmother Board of Trustees.
[1. Fairy tales. 2. Princesses—Fiction. 3. Beauty, Personal—Fiction.
4. Wisdom—Fiction. 5. Magic—Fiction. 6. Humorous stories.]
I. Cecil, Randy, ill. II. Title.
PZ8.G7495 U1 2002   [Fic]—dc21   2001039932
ISBN 0-8050-6847-3 / First Edition—2002 / Designed by Donna Mark
Printed in the United States of America on acid-free paper. ∞
3   5   7   9   10   8   6   4

For Judy Mittleman, in loving memory,
and for Hannah Mittleman, in joyous welcome

The
Ugly Princess
and the
Wise Fool

Chapter 1

A very long time ago, when all the countries you've ever heard of were in different places on the map, and the world was still full of the dark, wide forests where fairies tend to live, a princess was born who was not beautiful.

She wasn't even remotely pretty, and the whole kingdom was in deep shock about it, because in those days just about everybody was beautiful. All the written records from the era (they're easy to pick out, because they begin "Once upon a time") are filled with accounts of beautiful people. Snow White, Rapunzel, Sleeping Beauty, Cinderella . . . the list goes on and on.

Nobody really knows how to explain it. Some people

assume it must have been breeding: radiant princesses had been marrying noble princes for so long that the beauty genes had completely taken over. But that notion doesn't account for the millers' and tailors' daughters who regularly grew up beautiful under their soot and rags. Others suggest that the lifestyle was purer: nobody had invented cheeseburgers or smog, and everybody really enjoyed outdoor exercise, so they were hearty and muscular, with big square white teeth. Or maybe there were just so many fairies around that wishes for beauty were likelier to come true.

In any case, it was a world obsessed with beauty. The kingdom where the princess was born was called Couscous. It was closely surrounded by about twenty other kingdoms, and they had all been competing for centuries over which could produce the most beautiful princesses. The annual beauty contest had started out as a casual, good-humored affair, but every year it had seemed more and more important.

The contestants wore out their fairy godmothers with wishes, and then they tried tricks of their own. They glued on false eyelashes to magnify the starry brilliance of their eyes and dyed their hair to look like raspberry sorbet or Turkish carpets. Every child who didn't grow up as a prince or princess wanted to be a beauty-contest judge, because although the judges were supposed to work for free, they collected a handsome income of tips and bribes from kings and queens who expected their daughters to win.

So you can imagine how eagerly, on the night this princess was born, the populace of Couscous waited by the palace gates to hear tell of her tremendous beauty.

Chapter 2

And you can imagine the panic that broke out when the rumor spread that the baby, who had been named Rose, wasn't beautiful at all. Couscous's reputation fell sharply among the other kingdoms, and its own citizens' enthusiasm for paying taxes began to wane. Everybody was sure King Irwin and Queen Julia must be to blame, but nobody could figure out exactly what they'd done wrong. They were bewildered themselves.

What made everything worse was that Rose was the third princess. King Irwin and Queen Julia knew as well as anybody that they were expected to have three daughters, the first as lovely as the stars, the second as lovely as the moon, and the third more lovely than the stars, the moon, and the sun put together.

This was just the way things had always worked. Queen Julia herself had been a third princess, and King Irwin had competed with a thousand other princes for her hand. The two of them were traditional rulers who hadn't ever wanted to shake things up and were truly horrified to find they'd done so.

Of course, they were aware that the system wasn't perfect. It was rough on the first and second princesses, who were only born to build excitement for the third princesses and generally turned into wicked witches and flew away on broomsticks. (Life was even harder for step-sisters, who were expected to be disagreeable and stout as well.) Resigned to those probabilities, the king and queen had given their first two daughters the ugliest conceivable names—Asphalt and Concrete—and tried not to become too fond of them.

As planned, Asphalt and Concrete had grown as lovely as the stars and the moon, respectively. King Irwin and Queen Julia had rubbed their hands together, imagining how very beautiful their third daughter would have to be to outshine the first two. They'd actually

jumped up and down at the prospect of unveiling her at the annual beauty contest. Couscous would flourish, and tourists would come by the thousands!

After Rose was born, King Irwin and Queen Julia supported each other through the hard times by remembering the story of the ugly duckling. Then they sat back and waited.

But by the time Rose was thirteen, the maximum possible age for developing beauty in those days, there was still no trace of beauty about her. She had a wonderful character and a quick mind, and everybody liked her. She was buck-toothed and skinny, though, with freckles and hair cut too short for the glamorous styles that beautiful princesses were required to wear. Rose was always running, climbing, and riding bareback, and she knew that if she had to spend as much time on her hair as Asphalt and Concrete did she'd have no time left for anything fun.

Poor Asphalt and Concrete had such beautiful hair that they'd been forbidden to play lest they damage it and lose their edge in the beauty contests. Asphalt's black hair, described by the court poets as Clouds of Ebony Night, was a whole mile long. She had to lie flat in the courtyard for several hours each day and have it brushed by a team of experts. Concrete's hair, known as Wild Fiery Sunset, wasn't quite as long, but it was curly and got snarled easily, so it took even more time to manage.

Asphalt and Concrete didn't mind. They were so relieved that Rose wasn't a beauty who would force them to turn wicked and fly away on broomsticks that they remained sweet and docile. They had little to say for themselves because their heads were so heavy with hair. They looked forward to being married, when they would be able to switch to short, practical permanent waves, as all the local queens did.

"This is ridiculous," said King Irwin gloomily, watching Rose from the palace window one day. "The sun himself is supposed to marvel when he shines on her

10

face! And just look at her! Those teeth! Those skinned knees! Those . . ."

Queen Julia soothed him. "But everybody loves little Rose. She's so nice to her sisters and to you and me, too, dear. In a way, it's worked out very nicely. Asphalt and Concrete can have the beauty circuit to themselves and marry all the princes they like, and Rose can stay and be a comfort to us in our antiquity."

"Some comfort," said King Irwin in a grouchy voice, but the thought did cheer him, and he summoned his fool to come and do handstands.

Chapter 3

King Irwin was kindhearted, but he had an extremely simple mind, and his greatest fear was that wise men were making fun of him behind his back. When he inherited the Kingdom of Couscous, the first thing he did was publish an edict forbidding wise men to show their faces on the streets. Then, for good measure, and to prevent the wise men from figuring out a loophole, he also banished wisdom itself from the kingdom.

At that time all wise men wore long white beards, small round spectacles, and black robes, and they always carried leather satchels filled with important papers. They were easy to spot in a crowd. The other people in the kingdom didn't like the wise men because they used ten words where one would do but weren't of any use in a crisis, so nobody felt sorry when King Irwin made them stay indoors.

There, the wise men moped and sneered just as unpleasantly as they had done outside. It didn't occur to most of them that if they just changed their clothes and cut off their long white beards they would be able to go out in the streets again without being recognized. Or possibly they were so proud of being wise men that they would never have dreamed of giving up the image. The Wise Man's Academy had been badly managed over the years, and many of its graduates weren't really very wise anymore.

Except for one. His name was Jasper, and he was so smart that he'd graduated from the Academy when he was still in his teens, so his beard hadn't come in well and wasn't even white yet. He'd never gotten along with the students in his class, who had read hundreds of heavy, dry books and looked down on anybody who hadn't read exactly as many. Jasper had read all these books, of course, but he'd also read entertaining and juicy books that weren't on the approved wise man reading list, and he was curious about everything.

Jasper knew that King Irwin had every right to be suspicious of most so-called wise men: they really had been making fun of him. "That oaf Irwin," they called him, sniggering into their beards.

But although Jasper was as happy as anybody to see the backs of those particular wise men, he wasn't at all pleased that the king had banished wisdom along with them. He wasn't worried for his own sake, because he could get work in another field. What upset him was that the king was confusing the pretend wisdom of these men with real wisdom.

In Jasper's opinion, real wisdom was a rare and wonderful thing. A really wise person would never laugh at somebody for being different, or call a question stupid just because he already knew the answer. Couscous was sorely in need of some real wisdom, but the king had driven any hope of it indoors with the pretend.

Then King Irwin's fool retired, and the king started searching for a replacement. The main requirement was the ability to perform handstands. Jasper gave himself a crash course in handstands, cut off his straggly beard, and bought a cap and bells.

Chapter 4

On the day of the tryouts for the king's new fool, Jasper joined a line of extremely foolish-looking individuals standing on their hands in the courtyard. Every few minutes one would go into the king's reception chamber to be interviewed.

King Irwin had prepared only one question, which he solemnly read to each applicant from a parchment scroll. The question was "Have you had any education?"

Most applicants, who were truly fools, didn't understand what King Irwin was driving at. They assumed that he wanted them to list all the schools they'd attended and the books they'd read. Some even made up qualifications, claiming to be able to balance budgets and understand tax laws.

Each time this happened, King Irwin's face turned red, his eyebrows lowered, and his whiskers fluttered in the steam from his nostrils. He was so terrifying that each fool took to his heels.

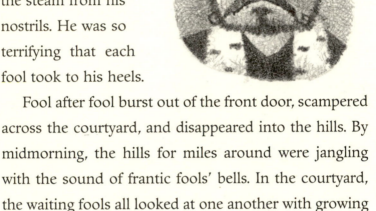

Fool after fool burst out of the front door, scampered across the courtyard, and disappeared into the hills. By midmorning, the hills for miles around were jangling with the sound of frantic fools' bells. In the courtyard, the waiting fools all looked at one another with growing dismay.

Finally it was Jasper's turn. He stood nervously in the reception chamber as the king unfurled his parchment scroll and asked, "Have you had any education?"

Jasper had to think fast. He didn't want to lie to the king, but he knew that if he admitted he had a Ph.D. in wisdom he'd never get the job.

"Thank you," he said politely. "I could eat anything. All I've had this morning is a duck egg." He pulled a handkerchief out of his pocket, tucked it into his collar, and sat down at the king's table. Then he looked around expectantly. "I just hope the education is not too rich, because I still have to show you my handstand."

King Irwin leaned forward, astonished. "I meant books," he said.

"Books?" Jasper asked, his face falling. "Those leathery pastries with the fibrous middles? I tried one once. I had to boil it for an hour, and even then I could only eat a few mouthfuls."

King Irwin laughed himself purple. "You are the biggest fool I've ever met," he said admiringly, and he gave Jasper the job on the spot. They got along beautifully, chatting for hours a day during the handstanding sessions. Without suspecting it, King Irwin even began to grow a little wiser from listening to Jasper's jokes, which were very silly and very wise at the same time.

Chapter 5

Not everybody was entirely happy with the new fool. The king's courtiers—plump, handsome fellows in velvet waistcoats who stood about telling the king that he was far too slender and ought to eat more sweets—resented Jasper from the start.

They grumbled among themselves about the amount of attention Jasper was getting, just for doing handstands, when they spent hours every day thinking of inventive ways to suggest that the king eat sweets. They knew the king truly hated one thing and one thing only: wisdom. So they kept thinking up devious schemes to trick Jasper into seeming wise.

"Jasper, what's one plus one?" a courtier would ask cunningly. Silence would fall in the king's chamber as Jasper collapsed from his handstand, pulled himself up, and assumed a wise stance, frowning and fondling an imaginary beard. He did it so convincingly that the king would begin to twitch and tremble, remembering how the real wise men used to look when he was a prince and consulted them on matters of state, and how they used to make him feel so clumsy and big-nosed.

The courtiers would watch the king and exchange unpleasant knowing smiles. Even if Jasper got the right answer by accident, the king might feel a little suspicious and look upon him less fondly.

"You're telling me you have two ones," Jasper would say. "Two perfectly good ones."

"That's right," the courtier would answer. "What do you get when you put them together?"

Jasper would think and think. "I deduce," he would conclude in triumph, "that you'd still have them both!"

The king would laugh anxiously and clap and indicate with his hand that Jasper should turn over and resume his handstand.

"Nonsense," the courtier would shout, flustered. "Everybody knows that if you put the ones together you'll get something else entirely."

The king would tighten his hands on the arms of his throne, puffing with rage. Jasper would shake his head.

"You can't trick me!" he'd exclaim. "If they become something else altogether, then you won't have two ones anymore. Either you have two ones or you don't, sir. You can't have it both ways."

The courtiers would be stumped. Slowly, King Irwin would begin to laugh again, triumphantly this time.

"See? An absolute fool!" he'd crow. "Even I know that the answer is two."

Then he'd turn a thunderous face to the courtier, who would see that the king was displeased and hastily say, "Then why don't you eat one plus one cookies to celebrate, my liege!"—as though the whole conversation had just been a clever way to surprise the king into eating more sweets.

"Very well—two cookies, then! But only two," the king would concede.

Chapter 6

Whenever the king went into the Cabinet, where he held all important meetings, Jasper had a few hours' break to rest his throbbing head. Usually he spent them reading on the side of a hill, far away from the prying eyes of the courtiers. If they caught him reading, he'd be thrown into the torture dungeon. So he had to be very careful as he scampered away into the fields, juggling for all he was worth so that nobody would notice the square lump under his shirt.

Then he'd flop down on the hillside and, after looking carefully over both shoulders, pull out his book. He read fairy tales that came in colorful covers. He read histories of ancient sandy places where when kings died they used to wrap them up in strips of cloth and put them inside pyramids with piles of gold. He read about the marvelous mechanical things inventors planned to make in the future: horses that could run without ever getting tired, geese that men could ride through the sky, and magic boxes that could cook five-course meals in the blink of an eye.

One afternoon he was dreaming of the future, a book open on his chest, when a shadow crossed the sun and an eager voice asked, "Is that a book?"

Jasper opened his eyes in alarm and saw a tall, thin girl with crooked teeth, a snub nose, and hair sticking up like a bristle brush. She'd been riding, and her horse was standing nearby. She looked about thirteen years old, so Jasper guessed that she was Rose, the youngest princess. She was no doubt a spoiled, spiteful thing who would delight in telling on him and ruining his chances of rescuing Couscous from ignorance.

But something about Rose's sweet smile convinced Jasper that there was hope. He looked down at the book on his chest with satisfaction.

"Are you admiring my chest protector?" he asked. "I often find that the sun makes this area of my chest too

warm. Then I had the great luck to find this foldable protector. It's exactly the right shape."

This wasn't exactly a lie, but it wasn't the *whole* truth.

"That's not a chest protector, Fool," Rose said, crouching beside Jasper and speaking in a whisper. "That's a book, and it violates a very serious edict. It contains wisdom, and my father has banished all wisdom from Couscous. You'd better let me have it."

She picked it up and opened to the first page.

"I know how to read," she confessed. "I learned in secret, so you mustn't tell anyone. It wouldn't look right."

She turned the page, and then the next. She forgot all about Jasper and read the book to the very end, and when she looked up her eyes were sparkling.

"I'd better keep this chest protector for you in my closet so you don't get in trouble," she said.

"That's okay, I have lots more of them—a whole crate," said Jasper. He was overjoyed to find somebody who loved books as much as he did.

"Very dangerous. I'd better have a look at those, too," Rose said, grinning from ear to ear. "Bring me another tomorrow, same time, same place."

Chapter 7

Everything went on happily enough until the day Rose turned sixteen. Up till then she'd never minded that she wasn't beautiful or that she'd thrown an entire way of life out of whack. She knew everybody in her kingdom and was the favorite playmate of all the local princes and princesses, her family doted on her, and the world was a big place to explore. Best of all, she was building a wonderful library through her friendship with Jasper.

But on that terrible day, Rose was sitting on the castle wall feeding the doves when she noticed a colorful cavalcade stirring up dust on the road below. Chargers charged, flags flapped, and horns hooted. It was the retinue of a foreign prince! He'd traveled across the sea to

pick a bride from the many dazzling local princesses, whose fame had spread to all four corners of the earth thanks to the hardworking court poets.

He looked like a conventional prince, the sort that Rose was used to seeing around. He had the usual square jaw and the usual piercing eyes, but somehow his jaw looked squarer than other princes', and his eyes seemed to pierce her heart.

She waved and smiled at the prince, who was craning his neck to look for any beautiful princesses who might be waiting in the castle turrets for him. He looked straight at Rose. A cold sneer distorted his perfect lips, and he looked away without waving. He spurred his steed faster, and the whole commotion dissolved into a distant puff of dust on the road that led to the next kingdom. Rose looked after it for a long time with a puzzled frown on her face, the first real frown she'd worn in her life.

That evening at supper, a messenger arrived with an invitation to a ball in honor of the esteemed foreigner, Prince Parsley. The invitation didn't mince words. "Only beautiful princesses need attend. No ugly ones. No scullery maids unless they're divinely beautiful under the soot and rags and have the appropriate footwear. You know who you are," it said across the top in bright gold letters.

The palace fell into an uproar. Rumors flew about Prince Parsley's vast kingdom and world travels. King Irwin coughed, wondering just how much education these foreign princes tended to pick up. Queen Julia imagined trips abroad to the exotic Kingdom of Herb. Asphalt and Concrete hauled their wilted heads out to the courtyard to be brushed again.

Rose found herself alone at the supper table. She couldn't go to the ball because she wasn't beautiful, and nobody even considered that she might feel left out. Jasper, coming to find her after a marathon of handstanding, was surprised by her wan expression. She refused to play cards with him and drifted upstairs to her bedroom.

Chapter 8

Rose sat down before the little dressing table that her godmother had given her. You haven't heard of Rose's godmother until now because she didn't live in Couscous anymore. She'd left the kingdom to travel the world with a sailor when Rose was a very little girl. "I hate to abandon you," she'd apologized, "but even a godmother's got to follow her heart." She'd given Rose the dressing table with its ancient and tarnished mirror as a keepsake.

It was a beautiful piece of furniture, but the face that looked out at Rose from the mirror was *not* beautiful, and that face was all Rose could see. She stared at it for a long, miserable time, getting sadder and angrier every minute. She forgot how lovingly her parents had always treated her and remembered every wistful glance they'd directed at her face when they thought she wasn't looking. She decided that Asphalt and Concrete had been gloating secretly behind their loving smiles all these years. Her friends, the local princes and princesses, were only polite to her because they were so well bred.

"They all feel sorry for me," she said. "Even Jasper's just nice because he knows I'll never marry. Prince Parsley is the first person who's ever been honest enough to let me know how awful I really look."

She stared at her reflection.

"I wish I were beautiful. I wish I were as beautiful as everybody expected me to be—no, more! I wish I were more beautiful than Asphalt and Concrete, more beautiful than Cinderella ever was, more beautiful than Snow White. . . ."

"Oh, Rose!" said a voice out of nowhere. "I'm disappointed in you!"

Rose's reflection in the mirror changed. It became the face of a healthy old woman, tanned from a life at sea.

"How did you get in there, Godmother?" Rose asked, but she wasn't as surprised as *you* would be, because in those days godmothers were almost always fairy god-

33

mothers and appeared at odd times, and most mirrors were magical.

"I know nothing can substitute for close personal supervision," said the fairy godmother, whose name was Eleanor, "but I gave you this mirror in case you ever ran into trouble. It can always find me; it's better than an answering service. I guess I shouldn't feel too guilty about going to sea, because it's taken you sixteen years to come up with a single wish. You've been happy."

"I'm not," said Rose sulkily. "I'm wretched."

Eleanor hit herself gently in the ear three times. "Did I get seawater in my pipes, or did I really hear you wish to be beautiful?" she asked. "Haven't you had enough of beauty in that kingdom? I don't see what's so great about it. Don't you want to compose passionate operas or be a famous healer or peacemaker—something that would help the world a little?"

"Being beautiful will help!" Rose cried. "I can show everybody just how they've underestimated me. Asphalt and Concrete will be so jealous!"

"I shouldn't have left you alone in that place," said Eleanor with a sigh. "All that attention to beauty could spoil a saint. I know from experience that wishes like yours tend to backfire. Fairy godmothers love to help goddaughters, but there are certain rules. One is that people have to accept their destinies. If they want to change, it has to be for the Right Reasons—and certainly not to hurt other people."

"I don't see how it's going to hurt anybody if I knock Prince Parsley's socks off," said Rose, but secretly she was imagining all the other princesses weeping as she whirled in his arms at the ball.

"Oh, it's Prince Parsley, is it? Come now, you'd find out how empty-headed that young man is after one conversation with him. Why don't you wish something really useful, like that the kingdom will get more cultured and clever and stop spending so much money on those pageants? The Couscous Ballet, for example, was always appalling—"

"Godmother!" Rose broke in angrily. "It's my wish, not yours, and I wish to be beautiful—more beautiful than anybody has ever been!"

"Do you know how many girls have made that wish tonight?" asked Eleanor. "We've heard from first, second, and even third princesses, plus many unknown princesses who've been forced to wear rags their whole lives by jealous stepmothers. Noblewomen of every rank have wished, too, and then of course there are the scullery maids. Our whole system is breaking down. Usually we give the maids priority, because they're so pure-hearted, but tonight there are hundreds to choose from. The fairy godmothers are squabbling like cats! You should have seen the viciousness in the pumpkin patch. I have seniority, so I'm allowed to distribute more beauty than any other godmother. You'll get my whole share, every drop, if that's what you really want. But are you *sure* it's what you want?"

"Are you kidding?" said Rose impatiently. "What are we waiting for?"

"I certainly hope Prince Parsley is worth it," muttered Eleanor, hauling a big kettle up from somewhere and sprinkling what looked like fish scales into it. "Because if you decide you don't want to marry him, after you've hogged the lion's share of the beauty, the other fairy godmothers are going to be pretty teed off. Wrathful, really, and a pack of wrathful fairy godmothers is not a comforting proposition."

With a loud *gloop*, Eleanor dropped something shaped like an octopus into the kettle, sniffed its aroma, and then began to stuff an oversized brambly bush in after it.

"One time a princess changed her mind at her wedding feast," she went on, after the kettle had reluctantly swallowed the bush. "What happened to her has never made it into the history books, because the Godmother Board of Trustees thought it would sully the image of the institution, but people still whisper about it. The phrase 'merciless vengeance' comes up every time."

"Godmother!" barked Rose. Eleanor had always been a bit talkative, and Rose was not in the mood to listen to her long stories. "Please. Can we get on with it?"

Widening her eyes, Eleanor suddenly vanished.

"Oh, Godmother, I'm sor—" began Rose, then stood, staring in the mirror.

Instead of Eleanor, she saw a magnificent reflection—her own face, but much more beautiful than it had ever been before. It was indescribable. Rose now looked more like a natural wonder than a human being. She equaled the sky, the sea, and the mountains in her epic grandeur. She spent all night staring at her transformed self and trying on the fantastic wardrobe that Eleanor, a practical-minded fairy, had also supplied.

Chapter 9

In the morning, which was of course the morning of the ball, Rose descended the stairs. You can imagine how the jaws dropped, and you can also imagine that certain people weren't very happy about this development—namely, Asphalt and Concrete. Even King Irwin and Queen Julia felt a little taken aback. For all their complaints, they really loved little Rose, and to see this blinding princess sweeping around the breakfast room in a newfangled turquoise cut-velvet morning dress was very unsettling.

The worst reaction of all came from Jasper. Rose went to find him as soon as she could, thinking that the lowly court fool would finally understand that little

Rose, whom he'd taken for granted for all these years, was a person of terrible importance. He would probably fall to his knees and proclaim eternal love—which she would have to spurn, since she was going to be Prince Parsley's bride.

"What have you done to yourself?" Jasper asked, squeezing his eyes shut and feeling around for a pair of sunglasses. So much reading had made his eyes sensitive.

Rose was indignant. "But this is what everybody wanted! Except Asphalt and Concrete, of course, but they've had it easy all their lives. Now they'll pay!"

"Ouch," said Jasper, squinting at her through the dark lenses. "That's going to take some getting used to. I was going to ask you to come riding with me, but now . . ."

"Who cares? Tonight I meet my destiny!"

Rose went upstairs to the princesses' dressing room determined to think only about Prince Parsley, his square jaw, his keen and hawklike eyes, and how pleased at least *he* would be to see her.

Chapter 10

"Well, isn't this a nice surprise?" hissed Asphalt as the three princesses, with the help of a team of experts, began to get dressed for the ball. "Just when we think it's safe to let our guard down, the kid goes and puts on the ritz."

Concrete's green eyes narrowed. "Sweet as muffins for sixteen years," she spat. "And all the time keeping *this* trick up her sleeve."

"Well, only one of us can marry Prince Parsley. Whoever it is better hope he's a nice guy," growled Asphalt.

"The Kingdom of Herb is way across the ocean, and nobody here is going to be in any hurry to exchange holiday cards," screeched Concrete.

"Despicable trick!" yowled Asphalt. "Sneaking, back-stabbing little . . ."

They didn't sound at all like the Asphalt and Concrete Rose knew. She'd never seen their faces look so hard and angry, or their brilliant eyes glitter with such

43

cruelty. Usually she entertained her sisters as they prepared for pageants and balls, telling them funny stories
and acting out plays, and they laughed and hugged her
until their hair got disarranged and the beauty experts
had to start over.

Tears came to her eyes.

But then she reminded herself of Prince Parsley and
how nice he would certainly be. She'd never have to see
Asphalt and Concrete again. They'd miss her, and they'd
be sorry for calling her names, but it would be too late
then! She'd be a queen. In the lonely Kingdom of Herb,
all the way across the ocean, but, still, a queen. Her hand
trembled as she attached her false eyelashes.

The three sisters got into the coach, noses up, not
speaking to one another.

Chapter 11

The ball was exactly as you've been led to expect. It was jam-packed with beautiful princesses. Prince Parsley was going around rating them with a team of experts, and you could see that he was getting flustered.

Each of the princesses was beautiful enough to make him an admirable bride. He could barely tell them apart, but he was terrified that he might pick the wrong one and hear later that there was a more beautiful princess in the region whom he'd somehow overlooked. He went from princess to princess, faster and faster, more and more greedily, leaving the team of experts bickering in his wake.

His eyes grew dazzled by all the beauty, and his heart pounded with ambition, and his mind felt cloudy and uncertain. By the time Rose entered the ballroom, Prince Parsley was on the verge of a collapse.

But as soon as he saw Rose, even he could tell that she was infinitely more beautiful than all the princesses he'd seen before. The whole ballroom fell silent with reverence and envy, and the spotlight shot right to Rose and stayed on her as she shimmered at the top of the steps.

Prince Parsley glanced back at the team of experts, and they all nodded their heads with great solemnity and gave him the thumbs-up sign. Then he glided thrillingly up to Rose, took her hand, and led her into a long and stately dance.

After a few minutes, the other princesses got their wraps and change purses and began to clear out. Asphalt and Concrete were disappointed but not entirely wicked yet, so instead of riding away on broomsticks, they hitched a ride from some neighboring princesses and left the coach for Rose.

Chapter 12

Back at the palace, Jasper was trying to resign himself to the sudden change in Rose's fortunes. He felt oddly miserable about it. Of course he would miss her when she was married and living across the ocean in Herb, although that wasn't the only thing that was bothering him. He wasn't sure exactly what was wrong, but he felt so gloomy that he knew he wasn't being logical. So he turned to something he'd learned at the Wise Man's Academy, which was known as the Wise Procedure.

First Jasper read all the books in his collection that dealt with third princesses specifically and third daughters in general, to make sure he covered all the bases. He jotted down notes as he went.

Here's what Jasper's notes looked like:

Third Daughters and Third Princesses

1. Not the sort who stay away from royal balls. Historically have always gone. Perfect attendance record—quite impressive considering obstacles. Are forced to scrub pavement stones, pick peas out of ashes, etc. But determination, local animals, and godmothers save day. Make gowns from commonly available household products, e.g., cobwebs and leaves. Arrange transportation in garden vegetables.
2. Suffer from inconvenient wearing-off of spells at midnight. End evenings sitting on pumpkins, lacking shoe, wearing cobwebs and leaves. Still do not call it quits. Often repeat whole thing twice more.
3. Wind up in distant kingdom, living happily ever after with square-jawed prince.
4. Are not friends with fools.

Next he copied his notes on the blackboard he kept in his room (which was next to the torture dungeon and quite mildewed, so there was little risk of anybody's nosing around in there).

Then he studied the blackboard, fondling an imaginary beard and keeping one knee bent and the other straight and one eye very widely open and the other very tightly closed. This posture was called the Air of Wisdom and was the most important part of the Wise Procedure. You weren't allowed to graduate from the Academy until you mastered it, and in the meantime you were tested on it every day. A professor would walk around and blow a whistle that meant you had to assume the Air of Wisdom no matter what you were doing, even if you were smashing mosquitoes or eating soup.

After studying these notes for a long time in the Air of Wisdom, Jasper drew a conclusion so unsentimental that his professors at the Academy would have given him the highest grade—L+ for Astonishingly Logical.

By acting so unlike herself, Rose was really just growing up and fulfilling her destiny. A person's destiny was something a fool didn't try to change, even if he happened to think she deserved more out of life. This destiny was carved in stone and polished by long tradition. And Jasper was only a fool after all, good for a laugh and a handstand but not much else.

He climbed up to one of the turrets and sat looking toward the brilliantly lit ballroom in the distance. Being logical, he'd found, did not necessarily put a person in a better mood.

Chapter 13

At the ballroom, meanwhile, Rose and Prince Parsley continued to dance, transfixed by each other. Prince Parsley held Rose in a firm, slightly wooden grip, counting to himself as he waltzed.

About an hour passed, and gradually the magic of the atmosphere began to wear off. Rose even found it a little spooky: the glaring spotlight, the empty bleachers, the soft waltz music, the mechanically dancing prince who never took his piercing eyes from her face. She cleared her throat.

"So, uh, it's Parsley, right?" she asked. She had the dulcet and melodic voice of all princesses, but it sounded loud because the room had been silent for so long.

"What?" the prince said. He was a little hard of hearing.

"Your name. Parsley?"

"What? Oh. Yeah."

"I'm Rose."

"Yeah, fine."

They waltzed a little longer. Prince Parsley's steps lagged, he kept sighing, and his eyes darted more and more often to the large gilt clock that hung on one wall of the ballroom.

"So what happens now?" Rose asked.

"What?"

"What's next?"

Prince Parsley blinked. "You've heard the stories," he said. "My counselors will consult with your parents to agree on a sizable dowry, and tomorrow morning we shall be married with pomp and style. Then we shall travel to my kingdom across the sea and live happily ever after."

"Oh!" said Rose. She thought. She stopped waltzing so suddenly that Prince Parsley skidded across the polished floor a few inches.

"Is there a problem?" he asked. "We're supposed to be waltzing, if you don't mind."

"What's your kingdom like?" Rose asked.

Prince Parsley pondered this question as though he'd never thought about it before.

"I don't know," he finally admitted. "Like most kingdoms, I guess. Its architecture is quite impressive, turrets, battlements, et cetera, and there's a couple of fools around for laughs. What did you expect?"

He took her in his arms again and resumed waltzing.

Rose had expected a different sort of description, something that would tell her more about what Prince Parsley himself was like.

She tried a more direct approach. "What do *you* do there?"

Prince Parsley's perfect brow furrowed, as if he didn't have a ready answer to *this* question either.

"Wait around for my dad to kick off so I can be king and govern wisely and tax the peasants blue," he eventually said.

He dipped her with great technical accuracy but little passion, touching the ballroom floor with her glamorous upswept hair.

"But what do you do for *fun*?" she pressed, after he had swung her back up.

Prince Parsley shrugged his broad shoulders exquisitely

as he twirled her. "Wake late, play golf, carouse all night. Prince stuff."

Rose was very worried now. She planted her feet again, making Prince Parsley skid to a halt for a second time. He snorted in frustration (handsomely, of course) and tugged his silken forelock.

Questions poured out of Rose. "Do you like to read? Do you like animals? What will I have to do?"

"Do whatever you want, as long as you keep your

looks," snapped the prince. "Now, could we *please* finish our waltz?"

Again he seized her in his arms, gazing with an expression of tender longing at the clock.

His answer, although uncivil, had reminded Rose that she was the most beautiful woman currently on earth, and she felt a bit better about the situation.

"Just one more thing," she said meekly.

"Yes?" the prince asked through gritted teeth. It was ten minutes to midnight.

"Are you very much in love with me?"

"My darling, I'll love you forever," Prince Parsley said in a flat voice, as though he were reciting something he'd been forced to memorize.

"Oh, that's very nice," said Rose faintly.

"Yeah, whatever," said the prince. He danced with Rose until the stroke of midnight without saying anything else, then got her cloak, put her in her carriage, and went back inside the ballroom for a big glass of huckleberry brandy. It had been a long night, and he was relieved it was over.

Chapter 14

Rose hurried to the royal stables, where she threw herself in the straw, weeping, her hair in disarray (although still unimaginably beautiful).

She'd made a big mistake! She had no interest in leaving her family and friends and voyaging to the Kingdom of Herb with disagreeable Prince Parsley. But if she refused to marry him after hogging most of the available beauty, every fairy godmother in the land would get mad at her.

What had Eleanor said about merciless vengeance? She wished she'd listened more carefully.

"Do you think there's *any* way out of it?" she sobbed

to the horses, but they just gazed at her sideways with one velvety eye each. They didn't seem to recognize her as their old friend Rose. (They didn't, in fact. They were wondering why a creature with such a splendid mane would make those unmannerly noises.)

Rose sobbed facedown, then faceup, then on her right side. As she was turning to sob on her left side, a shadow blotted out the moonlight from the stable door.

"So how was it?" Jasper asked, leaning against the door with crossed arms, averting his sensitive eyes from her beauty, and sulkily kicking straw.

"Jasper!" cried Rose. She sat up, so happy to see him that she forgot about the argument they'd had earlier. "Jasper, you'll never guess—"

"Oh, I'll just bet I *can* guess," he interrupted sourly. "It was the most magical night of your life, and you're crying from bliss." He kicked some more straw.

This guess was so far from the mark that Rose went back to sobbing.

"No, not at all," she managed. "It was horrible." She blew her nose. "It was okay at first, I suppose. With the spotlight and the reverence and envy—that part was charming. But I could have done without the rest.

Prince Parsley seems to be kind of a dud, just as my fairy godmother said."

"Really?" Jasper asked eagerly. He almost leaped into the straw to hug her. But he told himself that it was foolish to leap into straw—or to conclusions, for that matter. Emotion, his teachers used to tell him, is the enemy of logic. Although he would be delighted to think that Rose didn't like Prince Parsley after all, it was more rational to assume, in keeping with his earlier deductions, that the prince was still Rose's destiny and that she was merely experiencing wedding-day jitters.

So he said in his most rational voice, "Don't worry about it, kid. You just met the guy. You'll like him better once you're settled down."

"Hmmph," said Rose. "I doubt it. He doesn't share any of my interests. Even his eyes, which I thought were so piercing at first, are actually kind of glassy. And he smells of huckleberry brandy."

Prince Parsley was sounding worse and worse! But Jasper reminded himself that he'd never been a fan of square-jawed princes. He didn't have time to go through the entire Wise Procedure again, but the most logical thing under the circumstances was probably to give the prince the benefit of the doubt.

"So Prince Parsley had a few drinks at the ball," he said, waving his hand airily. "It's stressful to have to pick the most beautiful princess the world has ever seen."

Then, without thinking, he added, "Though if you ask me, you looked a lot better before."

Rose's exquisite jaw fell, and her tears froze, sparkling like diamonds on her porcelain cheeks.

"How can you say that?" she demanded. "My fairy godmother gave me the most beauty of anybody. And you're just a fool—what do you know? Prince Parsley certainly didn't have any complaints, and *he's* been around the world and back."

Huffily she began to shake straw out of her hair, which reflected the moonlight in vermilion flashes that danced on the stable walls and stung Jasper's eyes.

Jasper hurried to correct the misunderstanding before she did something even more blinding.

"That's not what I meant," he said. "You look like everybody else now, only with a sort of epic grandeur never before achieved." He glanced sideways at her, winced, and sighed. "But I miss the face you used to have, which I thought was pretty nice. Every day I knew

you, it became more your own. I may be a fool, but I've seen a lot of enormous starry eyes. *Your* eyes used to be like magnifying glasses—when I looked at the world through them, I saw it in a new way. Now I can't find you in all the glitter."

"Jasper!" Rose said. She blushed and felt warm and oddly happy. Jasper had never said anything like that to her before. She couldn't help comparing these generous words—and their effect on her—with Prince Parsley's clumsy attempts at romantic talk at the ball.

But how ungrateful she'd become! After all, she couldn't expect every man to be as sweet and guileless as Jasper. Just the night before, she'd longed desperately to hear even one romantic word from Prince Parsley. And now that her dream had come true, she was finding fault with his style? He'd picked her from all the princesses in the land and proclaimed eternal love. She should be thrilled.

Still, to be fair, she reminded herself, the prince did have some qualities that she hadn't taken into account the night before. He was just as glamorous in a ballroom as he was riding a steed. But he also seemed just as stuck-up and unfriendly. Not to mention dull. She'd assumed that the two of them would be bursting with questions and answers, sharing confidences and dreams of the future. Instead, he'd seemed annoyed by her efforts to get to know him.

Of course, Rose hadn't attended many formal parties. Maybe they all involved awkwardness and constraint. She'd felt strange in her voluminous white satin dress and clunky glass shoes and heavy, sticky false eyelashes.

Maybe Parsley had been just as uncomfortable in his high-necked, whalebone-reinforced, blue velvet doublet trimmed with gold braid and elephant tusks. Maybe they'd get along better if they were doing something fun, just being themselves.

She imagined them romping on the hillsides together. Or, rather, she *tried* to imagine them doing so. She could easily see herself frisking and gamboling as she often did. But she couldn't picture Parsley behaving that way. Try as she might, she could only imagine him striding along in a perfectly pressed riding costume, his back straight and his chest thrown out, wearing an expression of profound boredom.

Anyway, she remembered with a start, she could never really be herself around him. The old Rose, the one who had frolicked in shabby clothes on the hillsides, was gone forever, and the prince hadn't liked that Rose. She hadn't forgotten the disdainful way he'd looked at her when he'd pranced so handsomely past on his steed. He didn't want her to be herself! He just wanted to marry the enchanted person Eleanor had turned her into, the loveliest princess in the land.

This thought gave her the glimmer of an idea.

Chapter 15

"The beauty isn't the problem, Jasper," she began softly, in case any fairy godmothers were passing by. "The real problem is that I don't want to marry Prince Parsley. I know what you're up to, but you might as well stop trying to convince me. It isn't just nerves and it isn't just that I'm shy or that we got off on the wrong foot. I really and truly don't want to marry him."

Forgetting all about logic, Jasper threw a handful of straw in the air and whooped with delight. "Good for you!" he cried. "Of course he'll be disappointed, but it's for the best. Hurry and send a messenger to tell him you've changed your mind, because otherwise he'll gallop over the northern hills with his retinue, expecting you to voyage together to the Kingdom of Herb and live happily ever aft—"

"Tell me about it," Rose interrupted glumly. "Anyway, it's not as simple as that. If I let anybody know that I've changed my mind, apparently all the fairy godmothers will punish me with merciless vengeance."

Jasper sat down suddenly in the straw, exhausted and nearly speechless, and put his head in his hands. "Wow," he managed in a muffled croak.

Rose stood up and began walking in a circle, muttering. After several revolutions, she turned to face Jasper.

"What I *can't* do is refuse to marry Prince Parsley. But what if Prince Parsley refuses to marry *me*?"

Jasper looked up at her with a frown. "Why would *he* refuse? He came here on purpose to find the loveliest princess in the land, and he found her."

"He found what he *thought* was the loveliest princess in the land," Rose said dramatically. "But say he comes galloping over the northern hills and I look the way I used to look? It could be seen as a test of his love. I had to pass a test to win *his* heart, so he should have to pass one to win *mine*. Isn't that fair?"

Jasper wrinkled his nose. "It sounds fair," he said. "But how would it work? The old Rose is gone. You can't get her back. And there's no way to disguise your unimaginable beauty. Prince Parsley has the finest team of beauty experts in this corner of the earth."

Rose thought for a moment. "Maybe my fairy godmother could help."

"It . . . er . . . could be dangerous to bring her into it," said Jasper hastily. "Your idea seems sneaky and is probably against the rules. And didn't you mention something about merciless vengeance?"

Rose stood up and began to brush straw off her satin train. "Eleanor is an unconventional woman," she explained. "Let's go up and talk to her right now. There's not a moment to lose."

"Er," hemmed Jasper, backing up a few steps. He'd never met a fairy godmother. Wise men didn't believe in them and therefore didn't travel in their social circles, and fools spent too much time standing on their hands to meet many people. But every fairy godmother he'd read about in his books had twinkly eyes and just *knew* the truth about strangers without having to be told.

What if Rose's fairy godmother figured out he was a wise man and blew the whistle on him? King Irwin would swell into a rage and lock him in the torture dungeon and never talk to him again, and he'd lose his chance to save Couscous from ignorance.

"I could just find something to do down here in the stables," he suggested. "While you go up, you know, and . . ."

"Please come, Jasper," Rose said, taking his hand. "I could really use a friend."

Jasper drew a toe across the dusty stable floor.

"Please?" Rose asked again. "I promise to do something for you someday in return."

"Well, no real need for *that*, I mean, of course I'll come, if you think it's a good idea," Jasper babbled. He couldn't say no to Rose.

As he followed, he warned himself not to do or say anything wise that might attract this Eleanor person's twinkly, knowing gaze.

Chapter 16

At her dressing table, Rose sat down and yelled for Eleanor, who finally materialized, looking disheveled. It was suppertime at sea, she explained, and she'd been skinning a halibut.

Rose started to tell her story. She had a hard time getting to the point, though, because Eleanor kept interrupting with questions about what the other princesses had been wearing at the ball.

"Shocking pink? Of course—Clothilde's trademark. We're all *so* bored by it. And the hat you mentioned— was it a sort of dragonfly that buzzed around the ballroom by itself? Oh, it *was*!" She let out a guffaw. "I never thought Brunhilde would get that one off the ground!

Did you happen to see Princess Koo from the Kingdom of Kohlrabi? There were no pumpkins left by the time Petronella got to the patch, so poor Koo had to ride to the ball in a lettuce. *Very* damp. Anyway, go on."

With all these diversions, it took quite a while for Rose to tell the whole story. When she got to the part about not liking Prince Parsley so much, Eleanor stopped asking questions and began to look very serious.

As a result, Rose found it harder to explain herself, and she spoke more and more faintly.

"So I was wondering," she concluded in the faintest voice yet, "if there's any way you and I could work out some sort of deal. It's not that I'm changing my mind about marrying Prince Parsley, so the other fairy god-mothers needn't be vengeful. I'd just like to test his love before I do. Surely they wouldn't mind that."

She spoke so quietly that Jasper couldn't even hear her.

"You don't want to be beautiful anymore?" Eleanor asked. She sounded exceedingly solemn.

Both Rose and Jasper suddenly remembered that fairies had been known to turn vengeful all at once, without warning. Especially when their gifts were slighted.

"Ahem," said Rose.

"You want to give your wish back?" Eleanor continued even more gravely. "You want me to reverse the spell
I cast for you?"

Rose took a deep breath and closed her eyes. Behind
her, Jasper held his breath and closed his eyes, too. They
braced themselves for wrath.

"Yes," squeaked Rose.

"Well, my heavens, this *is* a pickle!" cried Eleanor
good-naturedly. "Just let me get out my old fairy-
godmother textbook." Her head vanished beneath the
level of the mirror, and they heard muffled exclamations
and the crashing of pots and pans.

As they glanced at each other, pale with relief,
Eleanor reappeared, even more disheveled, and set
down her textbook with a thump. A cloud of dust rose.

"I'm really not supposed to reverse these spells," she murmured, coughing. "They're very severe up at the district. But let's see what we can do." They heard the sound of stiff parchment pages turning.

Although he'd warned himself not to attract Eleanor's gaze, Jasper was too anxious to keep quiet. "Are you finding anything?" he asked.

"It's been years since I was in school. Oh, good. Here's that chapter on loopholes," said Eleanor. She skimmed quickly. "How do you feel about kissing frogs? Wait, that's for a different kind of spell—apparently you'd have to *be* the frog. Marrying a terrible beast? But that's what we're trying to *avoid*. Hmmm . . . oh! Spending a year and a day in the deep, dark forest as the slave of a cruel witch? The witch is really a prince in disguise, so it all turns out right in the end . . . but no way of knowing whether you'd like *that* prince any better than *this* one. . . ."

"Anyway, we don't *have* a year and a day," Jasper reminded her. "Prince Parsley's probably gartering his finest hose as we speak."

Rose made a face and darted to the window to check for the prince, and Eleanor paged more frantically through her book.

"Look," said Jasper, hoping to speed things up. "I've heard my share of stories. When people haven't learned their lesson, that's when they have to do all those grim things you're talking about, take all those tests and go on all those quests. But Rose *has* learned. She knows now that it's more important to be herself than to look the way everybody thinks she should."

"Aha! Learning your lesson!" Eleanor exclaimed, flipping pages in the other direction. "Of course!"

Then she stared at Jasper. "You're not such a fool after all, are you?" she asked.

Jasper went white. She was on to him! She had peered into his soul and seen the truth! What could he do? If he retorted, "Yes, I am, too," he'd be lying. If he agreed, "No, I'm not," then he'd have an awful lot of explaining to do.

His only recourse was to distract Eleanor with an answer that was no answer at all, as he'd done at the fool tryouts many years before.

"You know what they say," he mumbled, clearing his throat and looking out the window as hard as he could. "To know you're a fool is the beginning of all wisdom."

"I'll second that!" said Eleanor emphatically. She went back to flipping pages.

Jasper let out his breath, and his heart slowed to its customary rhythm. Eleanor seemed to have accepted his answer. He congratulated himself on avoiding a delicate situation and reminded himself once again to keep clear of those keen eyes.

Chapter 17

Unbeknownst to Jasper, though, somebody in the room was still staring at him suspiciously: Rose.

Eleanor's remark had seemed like a lighthearted joke. But Jasper had turned so pale and flustered and answered so oddly that Rose had begun to wonder.

She'd always called him a fool, because that was his job title. He'd been around as long as she could remember, doing the things that fools did: wearing a cap with bells, juggling, standing on his hands, and lending her his chest protectors. But although she'd never really thought about it before, she wouldn't describe him as foolish. For one thing, she'd often caught him *reading* those chest protectors. (He always pretended he wasn't, and he acted so touchy about it that she'd stopped accusing him of it, but she knew he was.) He'd taught her much of what she knew about botany, including medicinal herbs, and pastry-making and astronomy.

How could so wise and good a person be a fool?

"Jasper," she said hesitantly.

Jasper's heart began to race about again at a dangerous velocity, and he turned from the window. What if Rose asked him point-blank whether he was a fool? He couldn't weasel out of it a second time! He was still worn out from the first time!

"Y'see . . ." he began, stalling.

Just in time, Eleanor let out a shout from the mirror. "Here it is! Chapter Nine, Section F. 'Learning Your Lesson'!"

Rose and Jasper scrambled to the dressing table.

Then Eleanor sighed. "Oh, fish fingers!"

"What?" they asked.

"I'm really not allowed to take back the wish," she explained. "Fairy godmothers can't just be casting spells and taking them back, like yo-yos. That's one of our bylaws. Otherwise, you know people, they'd be asking for this, and then saying, 'No, I changed my mind, I want *that*.' And we'd never have any free time. And in this profession you really need free time—you spend so much energy on other people's problems that your own relationships get short-changed. Godfrey and I live together on the sailboat, but I tell you, there are weeks when we barely see each other. I'm busy talking on the mirror, and he's weighing anchor or putting up the jib or casting about. I can't very well complain that he's working too hard, because time and tide wait for no man or godmother—"

"So you mean there's *nothing*?" Rose interrupted, nearly crying. "The spell can *never* be reversed?"

"Well, I didn't say *that*," said Eleanor. "But the thing is, you really do have to prove that you've learned your lesson. I can't just check the Yes box on the Return Wish Form without providing documentation. It says so right here, in gilt."

"But Jasper's right. I *have* learned my lesson. How do I prove it?" asked Rose.

"I'm afraid you'll have to take a Test or go on a Quest after all," said Eleanor. "A Test or a Quest. Heavens, it's all coming back to me! How I racked my brains to memorize that rule in school! We also had to recite, 'Schools are schools, and rules are rules, and never the twain shall meet.' My, that's an odd slogan. Surely that can't be it?"

"Ahem!" said Jasper. "Excuse me. Which is quicker, a Test or a Quest? We don't have a lot of time."

Outside the window, the edges of the hills were just beginning to brighten with a new day.

Chapter 18

"Which is quicker, you ask?" mused Eleanor. "Well, let's see."

She consulted the index. She did this with such deliberation that Jasper began to tap his feet, scratch his nose and ears, and shake his head back and forth. He turned over into a handstand and then back onto his feet.

Painstakingly, Eleanor turned to the right page, smoothed it down with a ruler, and placed a whale-shaped brass paperweight on it. Then she set about reading it, following the words with her forefinger and mumbling to herself as she went.

"Here we go, time frames and scheduling. My, how complex—where on earth are my spectacles? Oh, right on top of my head, how silly of me. Here we go, then. A twinkling . . . a trice . . . seven years . . . one hundred years! Well, that certainly wouldn't . . . oh, I see, but only if a gnome is involved. . . ."

At last she looked up, satisfied: "The Test is quicker than the Quest. It takes fifteen minutes, tops."

"Then Rose should take the Test," said Jasper. "Don't you think so, Rose?"

"However," continued Eleanor, turning to another page, smoothing *it* with a ruler, and placing the paperweight on *it*, "the Test is harder than the Quest. Far, far harder, and in many ways more cruel. Once upon a time, there was a princess who opted for the Test. . . ." She pushed her spectacles back onto the crown of her head and sank back into the fuzzy recesses of the mirror as though she were about to tell a very long story.

Jasper spun around three times on his heels like a top.

"She'll take the Quest, then," he said.

He'd forgotten all about the Wise Procedure and was just guessing at this point.

"Oh, you'd like a Quest, would you?" Eleanor repeated thoughtfully. "Well, in many ways that *is* the

best bet. Rose merely has to do something impossible, like outwit a hungry ogre or avoid being burned to a crisp by a dragon or enchanted by a sorceress or trampled by a giant. And I have to say that the people who choose Quests always do admirably. It takes one hundred and fifty years, give or take a few, but it's a walk in the park compared with the Test, which, although it's multiple choice, can be quite tricky."

Jasper, who had been spinning on his heels during the entire length of this speech, came to a wobbly halt.

"Wait a second," he said shrewdly. "You're telling me that the Quest takes a hundred and fifty years and involves the risk of being eaten, burned to a crisp, enchanted, or trampled?" (Now he'd forgotten to act like a fool and was debating vigorously as though he were still at the Wise Man's Academy.)

"Yes. Why?" asked Eleanor innocently.

Jasper glowered at her. "And in contrast, the Test takes fifteen minutes and consists of multiple-choice questions?"

"In a manner of speaking," Eleanor said. "More like one yes-or-no question, really. But it's a doozy."

"That settles it," Jasper said. "Rose should definitely take the Test."

"All right, then," Eleanor answered. "I don't know why you didn't just say so to begin with. For a former wise man, you're rather indecisive."

Jasper jumped halfway out of his skin. Eleanor had just called him a former wise man in front of Rose!

But Rose, sitting at the dressing table and gazing in the mirror, did not appear to be listening.

Chapter 19

Rose hadn't actually been following the conversation for quite a while. She'd paid close attention at first, watching Eleanor in the mirror and listening to the discussion about Tests and Quests.

From time to time, she'd glimpsed fragments of her own reflection in the parts of the mirror that were not taken up by Eleanor's large, windblown hairdo.

She'd spotted a vermilion curl, then an amber eye, then a lip as tender as a newly blossomed rose petal. Each bit was so attractive that she wanted to look again.

Soon she was shifting around and bobbing her head, trying to find a free patch of mirror that would reflect a larger piece of her.

Just then Eleanor moved to the left, and Rose saw her own face reflected in full. She hadn't really looked at it since before the ball, and she'd forgotten how delicious it was. She pinched her cheek, firm and supple as a new plum, to make sure that it really belonged to her. She turned to the side. Any heart would break at the purity of her profile.

Her hair was still a mess from all that weeping in the straw, though. She picked up a brush and ran it through the cascading locks.

Ooooh! The hair responded beautifully to brushing! Her old hair had been uncooperative as a briar bush, and she and her mother had shed many tears over it together before they agreed to defy *The Third Princess Etiquette Book* and lop it all off.

But the new hair almost seemed to lift the brush out of her inexpert hand and guide it down to its own ends. It sighed and crackled with each stroke, growing softer, silkier, and shinier, clinging to her cheeks and whispering in her ears.

The whispers sounded like hundreds of sweet, eager voices, as though each strand were alive and calling out styling suggestions. "We'd look great in a pompadour! Try us in a French twist!"

Rose had always been intimidated by Asphalt's and Concrete's complex hairdos. She'd never forgotten the only time she'd tried to put up her hair all by herself. After several hours of red-faced wrestling, her hands going numb from being above her head for so long, she'd managed to form a hornlike protrusion that stuck straight in the air. Never again, she'd vowed.

But this hair seemed so helpful. Maybe she could try something simple yet sophisticated—for example, the look that was all the rage on the beauty-contest circuit these days, the Abyssinian Sheeptail.

As soon as she'd thought these words, her hair began to move by itself! Sheets of it flowed like water, smoothed themselves tightly against the sides of her head, knitted themselves together behind her, and then curled up into a vermilion crescent at the nape of her neck. She looked exactly like an unusually beautiful Abyssinian sheep.

Her hair was enchanted!

Rose sat and stared. This hair trick was too good to keep to herself. She ought to alert the court poets. They could whip up a sonnet and distribute it to the four corners of the earth by morning. It could be called "Third Princess's Hair Magical, Will Save Kingdom Bundle on Beauticians." Or something more lyrical that conveyed the same message.

Just as she was thinking this, Jasper, who had finished the negotiations described in the previous chapter, tapped her on the shoulder.

"Yes?" Rose asked irritably. She didn't even look up from the mirror. "May I help you?"

Chapter 20

"We're running out of time," Jasper said. "I think you should take the Test, because it's quicker, but even so there's not a moment to—"

"Test?" asked Rose.

Eleanor was watching them from the mirror with raised eyebrows, apparently trying to stay out of it.

Jasper snorted in Rose's ear, whiffling a lock of her hair with his breath.

"Yes, the Test," he hissed, whiffling another. "The Test you need to take before you can give this blasted beauty back."

With those three explosive Bs, he whiffled a deep furrow in the silken tresses above Rose's ear. The disarrayed strands whimpered softly in dismay and struggled to right themselves.

"Jasper!" Rose whined. "You've ruined my Sheeptail. Now I'll just have to start over."

"Your sheep *what*?" said Jasper, who, like many court fools of his era, was not an expert in women's fashions.

"My hairdo," said Rose, unraveling the tight curls.

"You don't mean to tell me you're doing your hair at a time like this? It's nearly morning, and Eleanor says this Test is very hard."

"What I'd really like to try," said Rose, "is something I saw at a beauty contest last year. I think it was called the Manta Ray Flip."

"Oh, the Manta Ray Flip?" said Eleanor, getting interested in spite of herself. "A girl I met at sea tried that once. She had to tie her hair to the half-mast to keep it up. For four days and four nights she stood out on the deck, until a strong wind came, and neither she nor her hair was ever seen again. *Very* impractical."

Rose smiled smugly. "Maybe for most hair, but not for mine! What do you say, hair?"

Before she'd even finished asking, the hair was shaking out its kinks and rising into two great wings that spanned the room. Then the end of each wing curled up in a perfect flip.

"What in Couscous is going on?" demanded Jasper, sounding strangely like King Irwin after he'd had too many sweets. "I've never seen hair do that before."

"Isn't it wonderful?" breathed Rose, patting the trembling gossamer wings.

Jasper looked at Eleanor suspiciously. She gazed back with studied innocence. She was up to something, he was sure of it.

While he'd been distracted by the argument about Tests and Quests, Eleanor must have put another spell on Rose, making her fall in love with her admittedly impressive and versatile hair. But why would Eleanor do such a thing? Wasn't she supposed to look out for Rose's interests?

"Now do an Antelope Horn Twist," Rose commanded the hair. "And then a Carp Fin. And then, just for fun, a Lightning Bolt Pompadour. The tallest you can muster. I want it licking the ceiling! Go, hair!"

Chapter 21

Jasper rubbed his imaginary beard for all he was worth. Was his wise-manhood so rusty from disuse that he had become a true fool, in essence as well as in name? He had to think of a new plan. The night outside the window was no longer velvety and black. It was a pale and unconvincing night—indeed, far more like a day.

Inside the room, things looked even more ominous. Rose's hair was zipping around her head like a nest of serpents as she shouted out orders and Eleanor cheered.

"Rose!" he yelled over the hubbub. "If you're still beautiful when the prince comes galloping over the northern hills with his retinue, he'll have no reason to refuse to marry you, and next thing you know you'll be voyaging to the Kingdom of Herb."

"Oh!" said Rose, jumping. She still didn't want to marry Prince Parsley. But was giving back the beauty really the only way out?

As she wondered, the hair formed a step pyramid from the top of her head all the way down to the floor, in perfect right angles. It was a stunning construction that an architect would have envied. Then, before her eyes, the hair transformed itself again. It began to curl up, weaving intricate patterns. It embroidered a flower garden on her head, dancing with a thousand tiny butterflies. She looked completely different from the way she had seconds before.

"Couldn't you disguise me as my old self just to test Prince Parsley, and then switch me right back to this nice new self again?" she asked Eleanor. "It wouldn't be as if you were lifting the spell permanently, so you wouldn't really be breaking the rules. And I wouldn't try to marry any more princes, unless of course they were friendly as well as square-jawed."

The smile had dropped off Eleanor's face. "Certainly not," she said brusquely. "That wouldn't sit well with the other fairy godmothers in the least. They don't like tricks. We're risking their wrath even by trying to reverse the spell. Our only hope is to convince them we did it for the Right Reasons."

Rose sulked. "But it's not fair. Why shouldn't *I* get to be beautiful? Everybody else is. It was a mistake to begin with that I wasn't. It wasn't *my* idea."

She noticed Jasper's reflection in the mirror, gazing at her with grief and disappointment, and she looked away, annoyed. Why was he trying to spoil her fun?

"Can't change any of that, I'm afraid. There are only two options," said Eleanor. "Either you can stay stunning and voyage to Herb, as you promised, or you can prove you've learned your lesson so I can reverse the spell, and we can see what happens."

Rose looked at herself, still trying to ignore Jasper's looming, gloomy face in the background. Giving back the spectacular hair seemed like an awfully harsh punishment just for not wanting to marry Prince Parsley.

If she had the hair, maybe living in Herb wouldn't be so bad. Prince Parsley would be off golfing and carousing, and she could sit in front of her mirror and do hairstyles. It would certainly benefit her new populace. No other kingdom in the world boasted a

queen with enchanted hair. She'd command it to perform a different style every twenty minutes and charge
admission. Tourism would skyrocket!

"That's all very well for the hair," interrupted Rose's
arms, in stiff, thin, lovely whispers. "But what about *us*?
We don't have as much versatility as the hair, so you
need to adorn us in a manner befitting our radiance."

"Good point," she said. She stood up and ran to her
closet, where the wardrobe her fairy godmother had given
her was hanging in abundant splendor. Somehow it
looked less abundant and splendid than she remembered.

"No, no, these won't do at all," the arms complained. "Too many long sleeves."

Then her feet began to stamp about, dissatisfied with the selection of shoes. Her fingers itched for rings, and her throat cried out in a melancholy, swanlike tone for a diamond necklace.

Clearly, she needed many more clothes, shoes, and jewels. First thing after breakfast, she'd send for the royal couturiers and commission a wardrobe fit for the Queen of Herb. She'd take them all with her on the voyage.

How much room would there be for luggage on Prince Parsley's boat? With a retinue of that size, probably not much. To accommodate her new wardrobe, she might have to leave behind the old books she'd hidden here in the closet. She picked one up.

It happened to be the very first book Jasper had given her on the hill, the first book she'd ever read all the way through. She'd read it many times since, and she knew it better than she knew anything else in the world.

Rose softened. This one book could come with her on the voyage to Herb.

Then she looked at the others, with their dented corners and faded, well-loved faces. How could she leave any behind?

Her hair stroked her cheeks and tickled her ears, wheedling, "Put down the book and play with us! We can change color, too! No peroxide necessary!"

"Oh, really?" she asked, turning back toward the dressing table. "I've always wanted a blond streak."

"Not so fast," objected the arms. "You need to think about bracelets for us."

"And shoes for us! You know, you'll have much more room for shoes in your luggage if *no* books come to Herb," the feet put in.

More softly than these voices, in a gentle murmur muffled by its cover, the shabby little book was still calling to Rose.

"But why do I have to choose?" Rose pleaded. "I can keep all of you happy."

She could make room for a *few* books in her luggage, and she could get more in Herb, where wisdom hadn't been banished. She'd preen every morning to satisfy the demands of the beauty, entertain tourists at lunchtime,

97

and ride horses and read in the afternoons just as she always had.

"Ride horses?" shrieked the hair. "What if we get tangled in a tree?"

"What if you fall and we get bruised?" cried the arms.

"What if we get callused?" demanded the feet.

"And if you're going to be carrying old books around, you'd better wear gloves," her hands called up at her.

"And buff and polish *us*!" the fingernails added.

"And when you've done all that," her cheeks announced, "we could use a moisturizer. It's dry in here."

Rose didn't know what to do first. She stood and listened to this cacophony.

How had she become so vain?

At that moment, standing in her closet, she understood that her charmed beauty was so fascinating that it would leave no time for anything else. It had already changed her, not just on the outside but on the inside, too. At this rate, she would soon be as greedy and empty as Prince Parsley himself.

She marched firmly back to the dressing table, where Jasper and Eleanor sat, one outside, one inside the mirror. She spoke loudly to drown out the insistent whispering of the hair, the rebukes of the arms, and the demands of the cheeks.

"I want to be me," she said. "I'll do whatever it takes."

"Hooray!" cried Jasper. He leaped into the air and did three full somersaults before landing on his feet.

For the second time in an hour, he had the urge to hug her, but then he remembered that there was still a lot of work to be done.

"Now time really is of the essence," he told Eleanor. "Can't we get started right away on the Test?"

"Don't be a fool, wise man," said Eleanor. "Rose has already passed it."

Chapter 22

Consternation erupted in the room. Jasper stared and demanded logical explanations, and Rose laughed with weak relief. In the excitement, nobody seemed to have noticed that Eleanor had called Jasper a wise man again.

"I told you the Test was a doozy," Eleanor reminded them, beaming.

"It sure fooled me," Jasper admitted. He checked his watch. "When will Rose look like herself?"

"Yes, and when will this hair and everything else stop yelling at me?" wondered Rose, wincing and covering her ears. The formerly soft and seductive voices had become deafening squeals of rage and disappointment.

Eleanor, not one to be pinned down by direct questions, was still congratulating herself on her work.

"Isn't it just the most dreadful Test?" she asked Rose with ill-concealed pride. "I developed it myself. The main danger is that it makes your true character come out, and nobody ever entirely likes what she finds. Vanity, greed—even the best people have traces of them. I had to distract Jasper while it was under way, because the whole point was to make you decide *for yourself* whether or not you really wanted to give the wish back. And I had to exaggerate the charms of the beauty so that your choice to renounce it would really mean something to the Godmother Board of Trustees. Talk about temptation! I'm particularly proud of the enchanted hair. I've wanted it for years myself!"

She looked more soberly at Rose. "I know it probably seemed a bit mean."

"It was very tricky," Rose said. "But what I'm mostly wondering right now is why the hair is *still* enchanted." She winced as it broke into a bone-shattering caterwauling. "If I've passed the Test, shouldn't it go back to the way it was before?"

Jasper was puzzled, too. "Are you telling me that the

whole time you and I were discussing the benefits of Tests versus Quests," he asked Eleanor, "Rose was already taking a Test?"

"That's right," said Eleanor smugly.

"But in that case," Jasper argued, "you didn't actually give her a choice. Before she'd had a chance to consider both options, you sprang the Test on her."

"Nonsense," Eleanor said. "She'll have to go on a Quest in any case. The Test was just a preliminary."

Rose and Jasper exchanged startled glances, then turned back to the mirror.

"Did you just say I'd have to go on a Quest, too?" Rose asked.

"A Test *and* a Quest," Eleanor recited impatiently. "That's the rule. Right here in gilt."

"You said a Test *or* a Quest," Jasper pointed out. "I distinctly heard you say *or* and not *and*."

"Did I?" asked Eleanor carelessly. "I told you it's been a long time since I was in school. To be completely honest, I wasn't a very dedicated student. I could never memorize those rules word for word. It caused me plenty of grief. But if it's any consolation, the working world is much more forgiving than school. You can interpret the rules a lot more loosely than people want you to believe. . . ."

"Now, listen here," said Jasper, drawing himself up into a full Air of Wisdom. "This just isn't right. You told us that a Quest would last one hundred and fifty years, and we don't have that kind of time."

"Oh, don't be so small-minded," sighed Eleanor. "It doesn't *have* to take a hundred and fifty years. It depends on how good you are. And Express Quests are offered under extreme circumstances, although I'm not promising anything. At any rate, I'd suggest setting off as soon as you can. Prince Parsley is oiling his saddle to a high sheen, and all you two have done about it is exchange startled glances."

Rose and Jasper exchanged several more before they could stop themselves.

"But what *is* the Quest?" Rose asked meekly. "Won't you tell us that?"

"Can't, can't," said Eleanor. "It says so right here in gilt. All I can tell you, Rose, is what I told you when all these shenanigans began—you have to want to change for the Right Reasons. Now off with you."

"But *where*, though?" asked Jasper.

"And can't you do anything in the meantime to keep this hair quiet?" put in Rose desperately.

Eleanor grew fainter and fuzzier in the mirror. "What's that, Godfrey?" she called, turning to look behind her. "*How* many sea serpents? Good heavens! Get out the harpoons. I'll be right there."

"Godmother?" called Rose. "Eleanor?"

Chapter 23

Jasper and Rose stood calling into the mirror, but it was no use. Eleanor was gone, and they were on their own.

Rose's hair, noticing itself in the mirror, once more began wheedling her to sit down and play.

"Let's get out of here," she said. She took Jasper's hand and hurried him toward the door.

But suddenly she remembered that it was *her* Quest, not his, and that he might have something else he wanted to do.

"Er, Jasper," she asked shyly, "do you have the time to accompany me on my Quest?"

"A hundred and fifty years? Let's see, let me check my schedule. Monday, handstanding. Tuesday, handstanding.

Looks like handstanding for the rest of my life," Jasper joked.

Then he added, more seriously, "I wasn't very much help during the Test, so I can't promise that I won't act like a fool during the Quest, too. But if you still want me to come, I'd be honored."

"I'd be grateful for the company," Rose said. "And I'd owe you another big favor."

"No need, no need," Jasper said gallantly.

Then, to hide his pleasure, he got down to business. "Where should we start? Your fairy godmother wasn't . . . um . . . terribly specific," he added delicately.

He knew Rose liked Eleanor, so he didn't want to say anything negative about her, but he found the woman maddening.

"From what I've read about Quests," Rose said, dropping her voice on the word *read* out of long habit (though the king's courtiers seldom got out of bed before noon), "you're just supposed to set off on them. Then things happen to you on the way."

"On the way *where*, though?" Jasper asked again. "We really don't have the time to be dilly-dallying." He sighed. "I guess I'm just not comfortable with this unstructured approach. I wish I knew the rules."

"But you don't," Rose reminded him gently. "And neither do I. So we'll just have to see what happens."

She felt sorry for Jasper, who was so sweet to try to help and so baffled by Eleanor's quirky ways.

Then she had a thought. "You know what might really be useful?" she asked in a casual tone. "A chest protector or two. The sun's about to come up, and it could be pretty bright out there on the Quest. Especially if we're gone for a hundred and fifty years. Do you happen to have any particularly sturdy chest protectors you could bring along? Mine are all a bit worn."

Jasper's eyes lit up. The prospect of taking reference materials with him made him feel more in control. "Good idea," he said. "I'll get the boo—er—chest protectors and meet you by the front portcullis."

He went down to his room beside the torture dungeon and drew from his secret library several highly regarded, heavily annotated volumes on Quests.

Chapter 24

As they set off together across the drawbridge, Jasper paged through one of his books in the dim light of dawn, pretending to be using it as a fan to cool his neck. But in fact he was skimming it for rules and tips.

"It occurs to me," he said when he reached page five, "that the woods might be a good place to start."

"Okay," said Rose.

When they got to the woods, the first thing Jasper did was bump into a tree, because he'd been furtively reading and not paying attention to where he was going.

But he recovered and led them on, and soon enough they reached a little path that wound through the woods along a stream.

"Yes, yes, this is exactly as it should be," Jasper murmured, comparing the scenery to the diagram on page fourteen. ". . . I guess," he added after a minute.

He stopped beside a large rock and then looked down the path as far as he could in either direction.

"Do you see any sort of sorcerer or witch?" he asked Rose, who obligingly began to look both ways down the path, too. "Keep in mind that they're often in disguise. One should be coming along any second, according to this . . . uh . . . sudden feeling I have."

"Right," Rose said. "But there's nobody here."

"True," agreed Jasper.

He pretended to gaze pensively off into the distance, but really he was trying to read page fifteen. He tilted his head to the side and tucked his chin tightly against his collarbone and looked down his nose at the book. The strain of this posture gave him a crick in the neck.

"We might as well sit down and wait," he said eventually. "My head is beginning to hurt."

"I'm not surprised," said Rose.

Jasper wondered what she meant by *that* but decided not to ask. They sat down on the rock and waited.

Jasper read up to page eighteen. Rose watched him.

"Can I borrow that chest protector?" she asked after a little while.

"This one?" Jasper suggested, offering her the second book he'd brought.

"No."

"This one?" Jasper asked, less hopefully, holding out the third book.

"No," Rose repeated in a patient but firm voice. "The one you've got open. Right there. On your lap. Yes, that one." She pointed at it.

There were no more books he could offer her instead. Still Jasper hesitated.

"I'll give it right back," Rose promised.

Reluctantly, Jasper handed it over. He sat fidgeting, with an unhappy feeling in his stomach, as Rose flipped to the beginning of the book and began to read the pages he'd just read.

"Did you read this paragraph on page thirteen?" she asked after a while.

"Hmmm?" he asked, pretending not to understand what she was talking about.

"You must not have noticed it," Rose said. "It says that before you do anything else on a Quest you should dig a deep hole under a pumpernickel tree."

"Let *me* see that!" Jasper said, snatching the book back. He held it right up to his eyes and read the paragraph top to bottom in two seconds.

"No, no, that won't work," he argued. He flipped back to page twelve and pointed out another passage. "See? Right here, it says you dig under the pumpernickel tree *only* if you're on a Quest for Buried Treasure."

Then he dropped the book and stared at Rose in horror.

"I . . . er . . . assume," he concluded weakly.

"Jasper," said Rose in a severe voice, "you know how to read, don't you?"

"I must have picked it up somehow. Don't tell your dad! I'd lose my job."

But Rose looked at him even more sternly. "I think you've *always* known how to read. Haven't you?"

Avoiding her eyes, Jasper kicked a little pebble. "Yes," he admitted sulkily.

"I see. Why have you been pretending all these years that you couldn't?"

Jasper squirmed. "Everybody knows that reading is a violation of the king's edict!"

"But pretending to *me*?" Rose asked, more softly and ominously.

Jasper hung his head, feeling like a cad. He wanted to tell Rose everything, but he'd kept quiet about it for so long that he didn't know how to start.

"You're the king's daughter," he mumbled. "If you knew I was breaking the law and didn't tell, you could have been charged with high treason. It was for your protection."

This wasn't a lie, but it wasn't the *whole* truth.

Rose studied Jasper's face closely. "There's something you're not telling me."

"Sure," Jasper said, in a snappish voice because he felt so bad about himself. "There are lots of things I'm not telling you. I'm not telling you what time it is, or what I had for supper yesterday, or why worms don't talk. I can't tell you everything all at once."

Rose lost her temper. "Fine!" she said, standing up. "If you're going to keep secrets from me, I'm not going to go on this silly Quest at all! I'm just going to go back to the palace and put on a wedding dress and wait for Prince Parsley to gallop over the northern hills and take me to the Kingdom of Herb, where I *will* live happily ever after, because for all his faults Prince Parsley at least does not keep *secrets*!"

She heaved up her silken train and stomped angrily down the path in the direction of the palace.

"I wouldn't be too sure about that!" Jasper called after her. "And if he *doesn't* keep secrets, it's because he's too boring and square-jawed to have any!"

He stood up, turned on his heel, and marched in the other direction.

Chapter 25

Jasper had been marching for only a few steps when he stopped short and peered ahead into the deep, dark woods. He could make out a figure coming toward him down the path. Terrific, he thought. *Now* you show up.

Jasper turned, searching the palace path for Rose, but she'd already disappeared around a curve. He called her name a few times. She didn't answer. She was probably still mad. Remorse filled his heart. What if Rose lost the opportunity to complete her Quest because of *his* deceit and stubbornness? If he'd only told her the whole truth, they would still have been sitting on the big rock together when the sorcerer or witch person passed by.

He could at least try to persuade the sorcerer or witch to follow him back to the palace and find Rose and do the Quest there. It wasn't something they traditionally agreed to do. But as that wacky Eleanor had remarked, in the real world you could sometimes bend the rules you'd memorized so carefully in school. It was worth a try.

So he waited by the rock. The figure approached very slowly. As it got nearer, Jasper could see that it was an old man, dressed in rags and carrying a sack and gathering wild berries. Just the sort of person his Quest book had led him to expect.

When the old man got even nearer, Jasper noticed that he was covered from head to foot in berry juice, a patchwork of purple, blue, red, yellow, orange, and even emerald green stains.

"Excuse me, sir," he said politely, stepping forward and addressing the old man.

The book had warned him that sorcerers and witches

must be spoken to very politely indeed, lest they take offense and put spells on you.

"I know this is a bit irregular, and I'm very sorry to interrupt you so unceremoniously, but, you see, my friend and I, we're on a Quest. . . ."

"Friend?" asked the old man, looking around with a puzzled expression. "I see only you."

Chapter 26

Rose huffed along down the path toward the palace as fast as her legs could take her in the heavy ball gown. Every hair on her head was singing in triumph and suggesting ever-more-complicated styles suitable for a wedding.

"Muffin Tin! Inverted Doorknob! Wilted Plum Blossom! Duck on a Nest with Four Eggs! Cherry Picked on Tuesday, Baked in a Pie on Wednesday!" they babbled.

Her arms were also talking to each other, debating the merits of cloth of gold versus cloth of silver.

Her shoulders were insisting on epaulettes, to the consternation of her ears.

"Please be quiet!" Rose shouted. Her heart, unlike all the other parts of her, was sore and unhappy.

She was beginning to think she'd done the wrong thing by storming away. Jasper had been her best friend since she was thirteen. And he'd stayed up all night with her, helping her through an entire Test and the beginning part of a Quest. He'd even managed to keep most of his temper, despite Eleanor. She should be able to overlook his secret-keeping at least long enough to finish her Quest, which was, of course, the most important thing. It didn't seem likely at this point that she'd succeed, but she really wouldn't feel good about herself if she just gave up out of ill humor. She slowed, turned around, and started back toward the big rock.

Then again, she thought, feeling a wave of sleepiness, maybe it would be best just not to rock the boat with all this Quest stuff. It was quite possible that Prince Parsley *was* her destiny. She *was* a third princess, after all. Her marriage would reconcile her parents to all the trouble she'd brought them and warm their aged hearts. She'd eventually get used to being the most beautiful woman on the earth, lit by spotlights wherever she went. She'd probably come to believe that the enchantment was real and that she'd never been ugly. If she hurried, she might even have time for a few hours' nap before the wedding and related festivities.

Rose turned toward the palace again, but this time she got only a couple of steps down the path before she came to a solid halt. Destiny or not, she didn't want to marry that terrible Prince Parsley. She had to finish her Quest! Jasper was the only one who seemed willing to help her, even if he did have that peculiar compulsion to keep secrets from her. And even if he didn't seem to be coming after her, trying to apologize. And even if it would serve him right if she got married and left him alone in Couscous.

Wait! Why did she need him anyway? What if she finished her Quest without his help? Rose imagined his surprise and amazement when he trudged sadly back to the palace, expecting wedding festivities, only to find that Prince Parsley was gone and there was no further question of marriage. He'd probably race over, full of happy questions, and try to cozy up to her as though nothing had gone wrong, but she'd just nod at him coolly and then never speak to him again, unless he was very nice. She was entitled to a few secrets of her own, after all!

She stepped off the path and began to slog through the dead leaves and underbrush with determination, even though, as her feet kept angrily reminding her, she had no idea where she was going. Surely sooner or later she'd run into the necessary sorcerer or witch. She didn't have any books, but many princesses before her had successfully accomplished Quests without dragging books along. If she remained goodhearted and well bred and pure of purpose, she reasoned, she'd get things right instinctively. All she could do was keep moving and hope she'd end up where she was meant to go.

Rose walked for what felt like hours (but was probably only about thirty minutes). The woods looked remarkably the same in all directions. Maybe they were enchanted, she began to think, a little nervously. She remembered noticing something in one of those Quest books about magic paths that took errant Questers in all sorts of wrong directions and threw them into the jaws of menace. Also, her left glass slipper was biting into her foot, causing her to limp and the foot itself to curse her in the lowest and most vicious language she'd ever heard.

Suddenly, over the sound of crunching leaves and the complaints of the foot, she heard a murmur of other voices. Was it the sorcerer or witch at last? She darted behind a tree and peered cautiously around the trunk.

And whom should she see but Jasper! He was standing exactly where she'd left him, beside the original big rock, talking vigorously in a cordial but strained voice, apparently to himself.

Rose grinned with relief. So she'd ended up back in the same place she'd started, after walking so far and so long! Some people might have found this turn of events disappointing, but it seemed highly orthodox and traditional to Rose, and it gave her the happy sense that she hadn't failed her Quest. The path must have been enchanted! (Actually, she'd been favoring her right side so heavily that she'd made one large circle through the woods without realizing it, but she never would have believed this explanation if you'd told her.) Obviously Jasper was destined to help her, and there was no way out of it. Despite her earlier bad mood, she was very glad to see him. The Quest just hadn't been as much fun without him.

She was about to call to him when she peeked out a little farther and saw that he was talking not to himself but to a little old man covered with berry juice.

Trust Jasper to help her out, even when she was behaving badly! This old man was almost certainly the person they'd been waiting for.

Chapter 27

"Is it some sort of imaginary friend?" Rose overheard the old man wondering.

"No," said Jasper, a shade less politely than before. "I've already explained *several* times. My friend *was* here, but she left before you arrived."

The old man shook his head. "I just don't see any friend, my boy. If you'll pardon me, I have a lot of berries to pick. I can't spend the whole day discussing friends of yours who show no signs of actually existing."

Jasper had been having this discussion for the whole thirty minutes Rose had been walking in a circle, and he was so frustrated at this point that he almost let the old man shuffle away. But he reminded himself that according to his book sorcerers and witches often tried to annoy or goad people into forgetting their Quests. Also, the old man looked familiar to him, though his face was unrecognizably blue with berry juice. Perhaps it was somebody he knew, in disguise.

"Kind sir," he tried again, "let's not talk any more about my friend right now. I honestly don't mean to be rude, but we're on a rather *urgent* Quest. Time is running out. I know there are usually several stages to this process, wherein you try to trick us in some way, and we have to be clever enough to outwit you, but I'm wondering if, just in this case, you could agree to speed things up a bit?"

The old man stared and scratched his head with his magenta fingertips. "Kid, I don't have any idea what you're talking about. Maybe you should ask this imaginary friend of yours to help you with your Quest nonsense. I'm a hardworking man, with berries to pi—"

Just then Rose crashed out of the underbrush.

Jasper smiled from ear to ear at the sight of her. "*Here* is my friend," he told the old man, a bit smugly.

The old man looked Rose up and down as if he still wasn't convinced that she was real. "All right, then," he said grudgingly. "So you have a friend after all. What do you expect *me* to do about it?"

Rose patted the old man soothingly on the shoulder, then drew her hand away to find it drenched in juice. She wiped it on her white satin train, leaving a bright purple handprint.

"I happened to overhear," she said. "As Jasper was explaining, while we don't mean to challenge your

experience in these matters, or make a mockery of a highly serious enterprise, we have only a few minutes to accomplish a Quest, and we were wondering if you could give us the Express version. I'd be happy to compensate you however you like for this kindness."

"If you're asking for berries," the old man said, "I can't help you. I have to make forty pots of jam for a wedding feast by this afternoon."

Rose elbowed Jasper.

"How interesting," she told the old man. "That's supposed to be *my* wedding feast. If you help me accomplish my Quest, there might not *be* a wedding feast after all!"

But to Rose's surprise, this possibility didn't sit well with the old man. He narrowed his eyes and scowled.

"That's a pretty turn of affairs," he muttered, turning away. "My biggest commission in six months, and then they cancel it. Well, I have a contract, and I'll get my pay! See if I don't, you aristocrats!" He shook his fist at them and began to shuffle off down the path.

"Sir!" Rose called after him, with a feeling of despair. "Sir, we simply don't have time for all of this. Tell us what to do! Must we help you make the jam?"

Jasper was paging through the Quest book, but he found nothing about how to handle surly jam-makers.

"Why would *you* want to make jam?" the old man asked, turning in surprise. "It's hot, sticky work, and you're all dressed up to go to some sort of ball, although what ball is held at ten in the morning I don't pretend to know. No, no jam-making for you, missy. It's back-breaking, jam-making! I wasn't always a jam-maker, of course," he mused, squinting nostalgically.

Jasper and Rose looked at each other with renewed hope. Maybe the jam-maker was a sorcerer or witch under some kind of spell.

"Back in the old days," the jam-maker continued, "I used to make pastries for hungry little boys. Smart, hungry little boys. And of course grown men, too, but the boys were my favorites. Oh, the pastries they could eat. Ah, well, life goes on," he said. He turned away and resumed his shuffling.

He was seeming more and more familiar to Jasper.

"Then what happened?" Rose yelled after him. "What sort of enchantment were you put under?"

"Enchantment?" called the old man over his shoulder. "Imaginary friends, enchantments—what kingdom do *you* come from? There was no enchantment. The school was closed down, and everybody had to leave."

Suddenly Jasper knew why the old man seemed so familiar. He closed his eyes and hoped with all his heart that the old man would shuffle off into the woods without recognizing *him*.

Rose hadn't given up. "So you're *not* actually a sorcerer or witch of some sort?" she screamed after the jam-maker.

"I don't think he is," Jasper hissed urgently. "I think we'd better get out of here."

"But why?" Rose asked. "This is the only person who's come along, and if the Quest book is right, he *must* be a sorcerer or witch. And we can't let him go until we outwit him in some way, or he gives us a hint of what to do next. That's the whole point of the Quest."

"Rose!" begged the terrified Jasper, tugging her hand. He sounded shrill and unusually boyish. "Come *on!*"

At this the jam-maker stopped, turned fully around, and stared at Jasper.

"That voice!" he said. "I've heard that voice before!"

He shuffled back with uncharacteristic speed and peered into Jasper's eyes. Jasper tried to duck and turn away, but the old man seized his chin with a purple hand.

His berry-stained face broke into a wide grin. "How could I have missed it! You were the smartest and peskiest of the lot!"

He embraced Jasper, weeping. "Do you remember how you used to love my huckleberry bagels?"

"Hello, Abe," said Jasper resignedly.

At school, Jasper had been so much younger than the rest of the students in his graduating class, and so much more advanced than the other boys his own age, that he hadn't had anybody to play with. Abe, the pastry chef, had been his best and only friend.

He would have been overjoyed to see Abe under any other circumstances, but this reunion seemed impossibly awkward just at the moment. He stared worriedly at Rose over Abe's fruity-smelling shoulder.

"And then you stood up at graduation, and you said in front of the whole school that the reason you'd grown so wise at such a young age was Old Abe's pastries! I never forgot it!" Abe sobbed.

"Excuse me, sir," interrupted Rose in a slow voice. "What school was this, exactly?"

"What school? What school do you think? The only school they've ever had around these parts, a great one, before it lost its way, and a darned shame the fool king shut it down. The Wise Man's Academy, up on Forest Street."

Chapter 28

"Abe," said Jasper gently, "I'd love to talk to you about the old days, but I have some explaining to do to my friend here first."

"Explain away!" said Abe, wiping away his tears, which had made skin-colored streaks down his blue cheeks. "I'll just be berry-picking along this path. When you're finished, I'll take you to my hovel and make you a huckleberry bagel for old times' sake. It sure is good to see you, boy! It makes the fruit juice flow in my veins again!"

Jasper led Rose to the original rock, and they sat down together side by side.

"As you may have surmised," Jasper began quietly, "I'm not a fool at all. I'm a wise man."

Rose nodded, but she didn't say anything. Jasper went on.

"If you want to tell your father and have me arrested, I understand. I'm violating several serious edicts. First of all, being outdoors. Second, impersonating a fool. Third, handstanding under false pretenses. Oh, there are too many others to list! I'd be in the torture dungeon for the rest of my life."

Rose still said nothing.

He sighed. "It would be a funny ending to all of this, because my real crime is that I haven't been wise *enough*. I managed to get into the palace, but then I couldn't think of a plan. I acted like a fool, and pretty soon I turned into one."

"But what were you trying to do?" asked Rose, putting her hand on his arm. "What did you need the plan *for*?"

"Oh, I wanted to rescue the kingdom from ignorance," Jasper said wryly. "I know it probably sounds silly now. I thought if I could persuade the king that it wasn't wisdom itself that was the problem but the way certain wise men were misbehaving, he'd reopen the

Academy under new management, and people would be allowed to read and learn and think again." He sighed.

"But that's absolutely wonderful!" exclaimed Rose. "That's the best idea I've ever heard!"

"Yes, I guess it *was* a good idea," Jasper said. "But it's too late now. I blew it. Oh well. Might as well go pick up my regulation crust of bread and sit in the torture dungeon."

Rose wasn't listening. "I wish I could have completed my Quest," she said regretfully. "Now it seems I'll have to marry that dopey Prince Parsley after all. I would have loved to stay here in Couscous and help you think up a plan. I owe you a couple of big favors, after all. And I think we make a good team."

Jasper was staring at her in horror.

Rose noticed his expression and her words stumbled to a halt. "If you don't agree, of course, I—"

Suddenly a weird shivery feeling shot through her scalp, down her neck, and then all the way to the tips of her toes.

"It's not that," Jasper managed. "It's your—"

"My hair!" Rose exclaimed at the same moment.

As Jasper watched, the enchanted hair began to

shrivel up. It twisted, curled, shrank, smoked, and shrieked. In a few minutes nothing was left but the original bristly brown brush on her head.

And under it, staring back at him in surprise, was Rose's familiar freckled, snub-nosed, buck-toothed face.

Jasper was so happy to see it that this time he couldn't stop himself from hugging her.

136

Chapter 29

Back at the palace, King Irwin, Queen Julia, and Asphalt and Concrete were in the royal breakfast room fortifying themselves for the festivities ahead. None of them was in a terribly good temper.

Disappointment in the outcome of the ball had naturally made Asphalt and Concrete a little witchier than they'd been the day before. They kept eyeing the broom closet as they squabbled over who'd eaten the last of the jam.

King Irwin was cross because he'd been awakened very early by Prince Parsley's counselors to negotiate the terms of the dowry. His own courtiers had been too groggy to suggest eating sweets during the meeting, and he'd been too bashful to eat any on his own. And now somebody had finished the jam.

Queen Julia was saddened by the faintly witchy behavior of her two older daughters and the mysterious absence of her youngest. Also, running out of jam at breakfast time made her feel like a bad manager.

"Please, Asphalt," she said wearily. "You can have all the jam you want at Rose's wedding. We've commissioned a big batch. If she ever comes back."

"She's probably off double-crossing some other sisters," said Concrete. Her skin had developed a greenish cast.

Asphalt cackled. She seemed to be growing a wart on the very tip of her nose.

Just then a commotion erupted in the front hall, and into the breakfast room trooped a strange assortment of people: the court fool, Jasper; a mostly purple man who made squishy noises when he walked; and, still in her bedraggled ball gown but no longer unimaginably beautiful, Rose!

The family was astonished at this second big transformation in as many days in Rose, and they took some time to settle down and listen to explanations. But after setting Abe to work on a fresh batch of huckleberry jam, Rose and Jasper managed to get everyone's attention.

They'd figured out a number of things on the walk back to the palace. Rose's Quest must have been to find an unselfish reason to give back her enchanted beauty. Now that it had been accomplished, they were both eager to rescue Couscous from ignorance.

Unfortunately, though, after all that work, everything still hinged on Prince Parsley. If he loved her true self after all, she'd have to marry him—or else the fairy godmothers would punish her with that merciless vengeance she'd heard so much about. Rose suspected that even merciless vengeance would be better than marrying Prince Parsley, but she wasn't sure how she'd feel about things when it came time for the punishment actually to be administered.

Rose and Jasper decided not to confuse the family with all the details. They simply said that the return of the old Rose was a test of Prince Parsley's True Love. The family accepted this explanation at once. They knew all about the odd and rigorous tests of True Love that people often had to go through. (While wooing Queen Julia, King Irwin had been forced to run a three-mile race on ice, wearing slippery socks.)

In any case, King Irwin was paying most of his attention to the huckleberry bagels Abe was baking as a special treat. And Asphalt and Concrete were chiefly interested in whether Rose's beauty was ever going to come back. They asked after it several times.

"I promise it won't," Rose said.

They looked at each other. "What about your new wardrobe? Do you get to keep it?"

"I'm not sure. Eleanor gave it to me as an extra, so I suppose if it's still up in my closet it's not going anywhere."

The two princesses immediately dispatched a messenger to check the closet for the new clothes. He returned with the news that they were still there.

"I can't imagine that you'll be needing that ermine anklet," said Asphalt.

"And what use could you possibly have for cloth-of-gold hunting breeches?" wondered Concrete.

They had evidently been snooping.

Rose said that they could have whatever they liked from the closet. And they hugged her and became a tiny bit less wicked.

"I just hope you'll be happy, dear," sighed Queen Julia, who out of all of them was the most worried about Rose's feelings.

Then everybody waited anxiously for Prince Parsley to arrive.

Chapter 30

Right on schedule, he did. He galloped over the distant northern hills and up the palace drawbridge amid his customary snapping banners and flapping cloaks and prancing white steeds.

The whole effect was ruined, though, by Prince Parsley's fed-up expression. His one huckleberry brandy the night before had become many, and he had a pounding headache that sitting on a prancing steed was not making any better.

When Rose was led out to him, he stared at her for a long time.

"Do you always look like this in the morning?" he asked at last.

Rose lowered her eyes demurely. "This is what I look like all day long."

Prince Parsley turned accusingly to his team of beauty experts, who threw up their hands.

"It's a trick!" Prince Parsley exclaimed, and his steed neighed and reared majestically. "This isn't the same person. It is, but it isn't. Is it a spell? I'm not into princesses who turn to frogs. Do you sleep on a pea? Spin straw into gold? I don't have to kiss you, do I?"

Rose glanced at Jasper for courage. His eyes held such affection for her that she felt prettier than she ever had in her life.

"Nothing can make me beautiful in your eyes but True Love," she said sweetly to the prince.

"Oh, is that all?" Prince Parsley said, relieved. "Well, that shouldn't be a problem. I told you I'd love you forever, as long as you kept your looks." He checked his watch nervously. "So, if you don't mind . . . we have a rather tight schedule . . . if you could perhaps . . . er . . . transform . . ."

Everybody coughed and scratched his or her knees and elbows and pretended to be interested in the horizon, which looked the same as always.

The prince got frustrated after about ten minutes of this and blurted, "You're not changing. You should get yourself a new fairy godmother or something."

The team of experts sniggered behind him.

"What I meant was, if you really loved me, you'd think I was beautiful as I am," explained Rose.

"Er, yes," the prince said awkwardly. He cast several pointed glares at the team of experts, but they had no help to offer. He made a mental note to fire the lot of them the moment he got back to Herb.

"You see," he began, "the thing is, as the highly handsome heir of Herb, I have an image to preserve, and expectations to meet. As you know, I've come all the way out here to pick the loveliest bride in the land, and our court poets have written numerous sonnets about it, and so it would be quite embarrassing for the kingdom if when I got back . . . well, how do I put this? . . ." He cleared his throat and fidgeted with the reins. "You do seem very nice, and actually you're not necessarily bad-looking now that I see you up close. The hairdo is kind of cute, and you have a sense of humor and inner peace about you that are quite appealing. But, you see, you're definitely not the loveliest princess in the land any longer, and I just don't think my parents, King Basil and Queen Marjoram, would approve."

"Are you saying you refuse to marry me?" Rose asked hopefully.

"Er, yes, I guess I am," confessed Prince Parsley. He felt foolish and ashamed of himself.

Everybody stood openmouthed, not quite sure what to do, except Rose and Jasper, who beamed at each other across the courtyard.

Right at that moment, a thunderclap sounded. The sky split open, and all was darkness and smoke.

Chapter 31

But then the sky closed up, and the light returned, and a lot of coughing could be heard.

Amid the smoke, seven strange women had appeared in the center of the courtyard, holding scarves over their mouths.

"Why do you always make the smoke so heavy, Clothilde?" asked one ill-temperedly. "It may be a little more impressive to the mortals, but it's a *lot* more damaging to my imported silk leggings."

"If you want to control the special effects, Brunhilde," responded Clothilde snidely, "*you* can try to be elected Chairperson at the millennial elections next month. *Again.*"

As you must have guessed, this was the Godmother Board of Trustees, which hadn't assembled in a manner visible to humans since the days of Sleeping Beauty.

Besides Clothilde and Brunhilde, the group included Petronella, Wanda, Maggie, Flo, and, of course—but standing a little to the right of the others and looking shamefaced—Eleanor. She had apparently been interrupted while digging clams, because she was still wearing her oilskin hip-waders.

"I'm sorry, Rose," Eleanor said. "The Board insists on an audit. They think you selfishly demanded the lion's share of the available beauty before the ball and then got me to reverse the spell right afterward so Prince Parsley would refuse to marry you and release you from the bargain."

"That's more or less what I *did* do," Rose admitted.

Everybody looked at her with sorrow and reproach, and the fairy godmothers began to swell and flicker wrathfully.

"It was very selfish of me to demand all the beauty that night," Rose went on. "Any other princess in the land probably deserved it more. Any other princess probably would have loved to marry Prince Parsley. Either Asphalt or Concrete would have made him a wonderful bride."

She looked remorsefully at her sisters, who smiled sweetly back at her. In the process, they lost their last twinges of witchiness.

"And when I decided we didn't have that much in common after all and I didn't want to marry him, I cheated Prince Parsley and the whole Kingdom of Herb out of the beautiful bride he worked so hard to pick. For that I'm sorry, too."

Prince Parsley shrugged. "It's actually okay," he said. "I wasn't too keen on the idea of settling down just yet anyway—but don't tell my pop! It means I have to come back sometime and hold another ball, and that always sets the court poets working on a new batch of odes to send out to the four corners of the earth, and tourism increases, so maybe he won't be *too* upset."

"It's awfully good of you to react so kindly," said Rose with gratitude, "and I certainly do hope that—"

"Excuse me!" shouted Clothilde. "*We* will decide what is okay and what is not okay. And things are decidedly *not* okay."

She turned to Rose. "Eleanor has been trying to convince us that she reversed the spell not out of favoritism but because you finally wanted to change for the Right

Reasons. But we can't figure out what these Right Reasons are. Something to do with wise men?"

King Irwin's scepter dropped to the flagstones with a tinny clatter. He retrieved it, and then, deeply offended, proclaimed, "I can assure you, madam, that nothing of the kind is to be feared. No wise man has dared show his face in Couscous for the whole of my reign. I published an edict, you see."

"Well, then, we don't know what to make of Eleanor's explanation," said Clothilde. "Can you please clear this up, Rose?"

Rose stared at Jasper. To explain what the Right Reasons were, she'd have to tell everyone Jasper's story and reveal their tentative plan for saving the kingdom from ignorance.

But just at that moment a wonderful, fruity fragrance filled the courtyard. Everybody stopped looking back and forth between Rose and Clothilde and began sniffing.

"Jam's ready!" called Abe through the window of the dining hall. "Nice and hot! Isn't it time to begin the feast?"

"There will *be* no feast!" shrieked Clothilde. "And you had all better prepare yourselves for our merciless vengeance!" But she moved to the window and peeked inside just the same.

Abe had outdone himself, heaping table after table with fruity pastries and delicious hot, runny jellies. The other palace cooks had provided the usual wedding fare of oxen, cole slaw, and raisin pie. It all looked very tasty.

"Shame to waste it, though," murmured Clothilde, who was hungry.

King Irwin, who was also hungry, recognized a kindred spirit.

"Perhaps," he suggested in a strong, kingly voice, "we could continue this very important discussion after a bracing repast. There are huckleberry bagels. It would be our honor to invite such a distinguished group of godmothers to our table."

"Well, we have traveled rather far," said Clothilde.

So they all went into the banquet hall, where the townspeople, who had been invited to the wedding feast, were already gathered.

Chapter 32

Five hours later, after seventeen rich courses, everybody in the kingdom was feeling full and relaxed and unwilling to get back into the debate about whether or not Rose deserved the merciless vengeance of the Godmother Board of Trustees.

But Clothilde took her responsibilities as Chairperson of the Board very seriously. She rapped on her water glass with her magic wand.

"It is now time," she began, "to address the issue of primary importance before us tonight. So, without further ado . . ."

Rose's and Jasper's eyes met across the banquet hall. They'd had a chance to confer, briefly, on the way in, and sketch out a plan, and they both knew that this was their chance.

"As you know," continued Clothilde, who like many Chairpersons had rather a hard time getting to her main point, "the Godmother Board of Trustees is an institution of long standing and prestige. Perhaps it would not be amiss at this point to review the illustrious history of this valued organization, and to give thanks to several people without whom we would not be here tonight. . . ."

As Clothilde talked, Jasper crept along the wall to the tables where the king's overpadded courtiers sat.

When he got there, he leaned over and whispered just eight words in the first courtier's ear.

Then he scampered away into the shadows before the courtier could turn his head on his plump neck and see who had done the whispering.

The courtier, whose name was Cedric, jumped up from his seat. "What's that?" he cried, looking around very excitedly. Then he bent down and whispered in the next courtier's ear. The next courtier also jumped up and cried, "What's that?" then bent and whispered in the third courtier's ear, and so on. Soon one side of the banquet hall rang with the sound of courtiers jumping up, crying "What's that?" and whispering in one another's ears.

At this moment, Rose tugged on her father's sleeve and made a suggestion in *his* ear.

"Excellent idea," exclaimed the king.

He leaned over and tapped Clothilde on the arm.

"Excuse me, Chairperson," he said politely. "My courtiers seem to be making a disturbance over there. They mean no disrespect, but they are accustomed, after a meal, to watching my fool, Jasper, who *actually knows how to stand on his hands.* Do you think you and your party might also enjoy this riveting entertainment before we get down to business?"

Clothilde was a bit taken aback, but she could tell that the king was very proud to be able to make this offer, and she didn't want to be rude, so she bowed her head gracefully.

The king snapped his fingers, and out came Jasper, springing across the floor on his hands. The king hooted and hollered and ate sweets. So did the townspeople. Seeing that this was local tradition, the godmothers all hooted and hollered and ate sweets, too.

At this moment, Cedric looked around at the other courtiers with malicious glee and rubbed his hands together evilly.

"Here we go," they murmured among themselves. "This is it. Now we're cooking."

Cedric stood up. "Oh, Jasper, if you don't mind. Just a quick question. What's one plus one?"

Jasper fell out of his handstand, to general hilarity, and struggled to his feet.

"You'll love this," the king said under his breath to Clothilde. "Such a fool!"

But Jasper paused for a long time before answering. "I've rethought my position on that question," he said at last. "One plus one is two."

Everybody gasped, and King Irwin reached for his scepter. He was chewing on a caramel, though, so he couldn't say anything right then.

Jasper walked over to Rose and made a little bow. "Will you marry me? We'll still be two ones, but we'll also be two."

Rose blushed. This was part of the plan, but it sounded funny out loud. Before she could answer, Cedric interrupted.

"Would you have your third princess marry a fool, Your Highness?" he asked snidely. "Not particularly traditional, is it?"

"We can't afford to be too stuffy, now that she's turned down the handsomest prince on earth," said the king, who'd swallowed the caramel and dropped his scepter and was looking as happy as a large red king could.

"But you never did a background check on the fool, did you?" Cedric asked. "Background checks are Couscous policy."

King Irwin waved his hand. "A minor oversight, easily remedied."

"But what if the background check revealed what I have just learned on good authority—that Jasper is really a wise man in disguise?" (For this was the rumor that Jasper had planted in Cedric's ear.)

Silence fell. The other courtiers sat up straighter, their velvet waistcoats tightening over their inflated bellies, their eyes bugging out. The townspeople murmured in consternation, and the fairy godmothers looked at one another with increasing curiosity. More was going on here than they'd guessed.

But the king seemed to think it was all a terrific joke. He bowed double, laughing.

"A wise man! Jasper! Nobody could be more foolish!" He wheezed and pounded his fist on the table. "Figuring out one plus one after all this time hardly makes him a genius!"

After a little while, he calmed down and wiped his eyes and reached for another caramel. He happened to glance at Jasper as he did so. To his surprise, his beloved fool wore an extremely serious expression.

"You don't think I believe this absurd story, do you?" he asked Jasper kindly.

"But the story is true, Your Highness," Jasper said. He pulled a pair of small round wise man–issue spectacles out of his jester's cap and put them on. "I *am* a wise man. I know not only that one plus one is two, but that two plus two is four, and that four times four is sixteen. I know that the square root of twenty-five is five. I know—"

"Desist!" cried the king. "Stand on your hands this instant."

Jasper obliged.

"This changes nothing, Your Honor," he said meekly, upside down. "Not all wise men think they're too good to stand on their hands or tell a joke. In fact, even *you* are a wise man"—the townspeople gasped again, and King Irwin's face drained of blood—"because you hate false wisdom. You don't want people around you who mock others and put on airs. Neither do I. And neither does any truly wise person. I think it's time we gave true wisdom another opportunity to show its face in Couscous. It's time you let people read and think again, and reopened the Wise Man's Academy."

"Well . . . this . . . does . . . bear . . . consideration," said King Irwin in fright. He had no idea what to do. To stop himself from saying anything he'd regret, he stuffed six more caramels in his mouth.

"You see, Clothilde!" interrupted Eleanor, too impatient to wait a second longer. "This was why I took back Rose's beauty. If this isn't the Right Reason, nothing is! She wanted to help the fool restore wisdom to the kingdom. Don't you think that's unselfish? Much better than hoping to spend her life being lit by spotlights and doing her hair."

Everybody looked at Clothilde. She and the other members of the Board conferred for a long moment.

"Let it be resolved," she announced finally. "After one really regrettable lapse of judgment, Princess Rose was willing to sacrifice herself to our merciless vengeance, all for the sake of Couscous."

She looked around at the breathless crowd.

"And thus," she concluded, "no merciless vengeance."

Everybody sighed with relief, and there was scattered applause.

"But!" Clothilde added sharply, causing everybody to gasp all over again.

She didn't have anything else to say, really, but she didn't want to come across as too soft, especially with the Board elections around the corner.

So she walked up to Rose and looked her straight in

the eye. "Don't you *ever* try to bend the rules like that again, young lady! We fairy godmothers have a slogan, 'Schools are schools, and rules are rules, and never the twain shall meet.' You think about that next time you want to play fast and loose with tradition."

"Yes, ma'am," said Rose very politely.

Eleanor shrugged at her from behind Clothilde's back, mouthed, "I don't know what it means either," then winked and blew her a kiss.

All the fairy godmothers vanished together in their customary smoky thunderclap.

When the smoke had cleared this time, the banquet hall fell into delighted confusion, courtiers complaining, townspeople babbling, and the king choking on caramels. Jasper dropped out of his handstand and slipped unnoticed through the crowd to Rose's side.

They said hi, rather shyly and stiffly for two people who had just teamed up to rescue a kingdom from ignorance.

"So that went well," Jasper said, tying his cap and bells in a knot.

"Sure did," Rose agreed, polishing a flagon with the hem of her ball gown.

He chewed his lip, whistled, and looked up at the ceiling. "By the way, speaking of . . . well, things . . . you didn't actually answer my question."

"Question?" Rose asked innocently. "I'm sorry, I can't really hear you. All these voices jabbering. It reminds me of that enchanted hair."

"Ah, yes," Jasper said, laughing. He was glad he was able to laugh about it. Then a thought made him turn pale. "Do you miss the hair?"

"Nope," she said. "The hair was creepy."

Jasper smiled but didn't know what else to say.

"What about you?" Rose asked. "Now that you're a true hero, you could probably buy yourself a steed, rent a retinue, and throw a ball yourself. You could end up marrying the loveliest princess in the land."

"That," said Jasper, looking at her tenderly, "is exactly what I'm trying to do."

Chapter 33

You're probably wondering if everything completely changed in Couscous after that day.

Of course it didn't.

And you're probably suspecting that everybody lived happily ever after.

They did—more or less.

Cedric and the other courtiers all kept their jobs, because the king still liked being persuaded to eat sweets. The annual beauty contests went on as usual, and princes kept galloping across the land and throwing balls, and there was always plenty of demand for the fairy godmothers' services.

There were a few small differences, though.

Prince Parsley made history by voyaging back to his kingdom without a bride, and some people worried that the event signaled hard times ahead in the ball-throwing business. But the next year he simply galloped through the land again. This time he didn't drink so much huckleberry brandy, and he fell madly in love with Princess Koo from the Kingdom of Kohlrabi. They voyaged back to Herb together in an enchanted cabbage leaf. Everybody was truly happy for them, even Asphalt and Concrete, who had forgotten all about Parsley after getting married to two handsome local princes and cutting off their hair.

King Irwin reinstated the Wise Man's Academy with Jasper's help—although now, because women were admitted too, it was called the Wise Person's Academy. There were more stringent entrance requirements, and no dress code, and Jasper himself was put in charge. Naturally Abe got his old job back, making pastries for the students (he washed off most of the berry juice first).

After becoming the first third princess in history to earn her degree in wisdom, Rose finally got around to considering Jasper's marriage proposal. As you surely guessed she would, she said yes. They had a big family and were kept extremely busy, running the Academy and reading and playing on the hills.

They barely had any time to talk to Eleanor on the mirror.

But each year, to mark the anniversary of the Test and the Quest that had brought them together, she mailed them a smoked salmon.